SNOW MERCY

ALASKA COZY MYSTERY #11

WENDY MEADOWS

MAJESTIC OWL PUBLISHING LLC

Amanda nudged Sarah with her elbow on the snowy sidewalk. "Is this kid for real?" she asked in a voice that almost sounded comical.

"I'm not sure," Sarah replied, staring at a very short person wearing a black ski mask over his face and what appeared to be a rusted hunting knife in his right hand.

"I said give me all of your money!" Manford Sappers demanded in a nervous tone that he hoped sounded fierce and intimidating. Sure, he felt lower than an earth worm holding up two beautiful women in a snow storm, but he was desperate—and hungry. In fact, he was starving. "I don't want to hurt you!"

Sarah stared at Manford with curious eyes, realizing it wasn't a child at all. It was an adult man, just very, very short. Was the man a little person? The poor little guy was shaking all over—and it wasn't the cold or the snow making him shake. "I never thought I would get mugged standing outside of O'Mally's department store," she said in a calm voice and slowly folded her arms over a light pink coat that Conrad had bought her a few days back.

Manford quickly licked his lips, glanced to the right, saw only a snowy parking lot bare of cars, glanced to his left, saw the same thing, and then focused back on Sarah and Amanda. The woman wearing the pink coat sure was pretty, but Manford saw the woman had a hardened toughness in her eyes, kind of like a cop, which spooked him. The woman wearing the white coat was pretty, too, but had the eyes of a person who wasn't going to give over her purse without a fight. "Come on, ladies," Manford growled—a growl that sounded more like a plea, "hand over your money."

Amanda fought back a grin. The little man was very pitiful standing in the snow, shivering from top to bottom, terrified even as he attempted to mug two innocent women. "How about we go inside and buy you a proper coat?" she asked and nodded at the raggedy coat Manford wore.

Manford dropped his eyes, studied the black coat he had bought at a thrift store, counted the holes in the coat, and then sighed. "Your pants aren't much better than your coat, I'm afraid," Sarah pointed out. "And those tennis shoes on your feet look like they're about to fall apart. You're freezing!"

"Please...give me your money, huh?" Manford begged. "I'm cold, hungry...I ain't even got socks. My feet feel like ice. So...enough with the pity-party talk...hand over the cash!"

Sarah glanced at Amanda. Amanda shrugged her shoulders and then slowly adjusted her warm blue snow hat down over her ears. "Wind is picking up," she said and tossed a thumb at the glass door leading into O'Mally's. "Temperature is dropping, too. I think I'll go inside to the snack bar and get a hot coffee."

"Yeah, that's a good idea," Sarah agreed. "But first, maybe I should give this poor fella my wallet." Sarah moved to pull out her wallet and then dropped it. "Oops!" She slowly bent down and pointed at it. "Nice and easy, okay, fella? Just going to get it."

"Yeah...easy..." Manford warned Sarah. "No...no funny stuff."

"No funny stuff," Sarah assured Manford, watching his scared eyes following her hands like a hungry bear following a raw steak. It was clear to Sarah that the poor man was starving, which is why she hated to pull her gun on him. But what choice did she have?

"Hey...what is this?" Manford cried in shock as Sarah

grabbed her wallet and then also yanked a gun out from the holster hidden at her ankle. "You said no funny stuff!"

"Drop the knife," Sarah said in an easy voice and nodded at the hunting knife Manford was holding in his right hand.

Manford shook his head. "Trust me to pick the exact wrong women to try to hold up," he said in a miserable voice and then threw the hunting knife down into the snow. "You're a cop, right?" he asked Sarah. "Yeah, sure you are...seen eyes like yours in big cities."

"I'm a retired cop," Sarah told Manford. She slowly lowered her gun. "What's your name?"

"What's that to you?" Manford asked. "You gonna get me arrested? Call your cop friends? Cops don't care about names unless they're arresting you...until then, I'm just another thug."

Amanda grinned. "An attempted thug, maybe? Sounds like you've been arrested before, though."

"A few times," Manford nodded his head, trying to sound tough and hide the rumbling of his stomach. "I've been in the slammer before...all petty stuff, though...shoplifting, mostly."

"Looks like you're working your way up the ladder," Sarah told Manford in a serious voice. "Armed robbery and attempted assault is pretty serious. Could get you a couple of felony charges. Also...cops don't take well to a man pulling a knife on two women...no matter their size difference."

"Yeah, yeah, I know," Manford replied in a miserable voice and quickly wiped snow off his ski mask. "What I did was stupid. But hey," he added, "at least I'll get something to eat in the jug. So...let's quit talking. Haul me in already, huh? Call your cop friends. The sooner I get something to eat, the better."

"This isn't Mayberry," Sarah told Manford. "Aunt Bee isn't bringing you a fried chicken supper."

"Right now, I'd settle for bread and water," Manford said and held out his hands. "Slap the cuffs on and haul me away, hot stuff."

"Did he just call you hot stuff?" Amanda asked and then giggled to herself. "From a scared rat to a brave flirt. Oh, my...what a morning."

Manford shrugged his shoulders. Now that it was clear that he was going to jail, the desperate fear of his situation slipped off his shoulders and drifted off into the wind. Sure, going back to jail was scary, but not half as scary as forcing yourself to commit acts that put you among the lowest of the low. "Might as well compliment a pretty lady before the bars are slammed shut in my face. Might be the last pretty face my eyes see in a long time."

He grinned up at Sarah, shivering as he folded his arms together.

"Hey, what about me?" Amanda asked. "I'm not exactly a dog."

"You're a pretty face, too," Manford promised Amanda, "but the cop...wow, she's really hot stuff." He said this in a stagey whisper, clearly intending for Sarah to overhear.

Amanda rolled her eyes. "I guess we better call Conrad to come haul Romeo to the...jug," she told Sarah.

Sarah stared at Manford. "I don't think I'll bother my husband this morning," she said.

"Husband?" Manford gulped.

"Detective Conrad Spencer is my husband." Sarah nodded her head as a powerful gust of icy wind grabbed at the white ski cap on her head. "My name is Detective Sarah Garland...Sarah Spencer."

"Boy, did I pick the wrong dames," Manford said in a miserable voice. "Of all the places...who knew?"

"Just what are you doing in Snow Falls, Alaska?" Sarah asked.

"Hunting," Manford replied in a sarcastic voice and kicked the hunting knife lying in the snow.

"Or running," Sarah added. "What's your name?"

"Elmer Fudd."

"Oh, just throw some cuffs on this guy and call Conrad," Amanda begged. "I want a hot coffee to warm my legs up for all the shopping we're going to do, love."

"You're just mad because I think the cop is prettier than you," Manford snapped at Amanda.

"Am not."

"Are too," Manford insisted and stuck his tongue out at Amanda.

"I'll tie your tongue in a knot, you bloody little..." Amanda charged at Manford. Manford nearly jumped out of his skin, stumbled backward, tripped, and landed on his butt.

Sarah gently touched Amanda's arm to hold her back. "Why don't you go inside and order three coffees and..." she looked down at Manford, studied his hungry eyes, and nodded her head, "as many cheeseburgers as you can."

Amanda locked her gaze on Manford. She had to admit the little guy was in need of some serious help. Even if he had a mouth on him, and an attitude to boot. "Okay, love. And after we feed him, we'll buy the guy some proper winter clothing. I know they carry big and tall sizes... maybe they also carry short and mouthy! What do you say, short stuff?"

"Cheeseburgers...winter clothing?" Manford asked. "What are you talking about? Aren't you taking me to the jug?"

"Nope," Sarah smiled and then, to Manford's shock, put her gun away. "Seems to me that once we get some food in your belly and get you warmed up, we'll be able to get you to talk some."

Manford couldn't believe his ears. Was Sarah for real? He wasn't sure. "Hey," he protested and ripped off his ski mask, revealing messy brown hair falling over a handsome face that couldn't have been older than twenty-five years, "I don't need no charity. Manford Sappers makes it on his own."

"State-funded jail food isn't making it on your own," Sarah pointed out. "Neither is stealing money from two women. Making it on your own means working hard, staying honest, paying your bills, and buying things with money you've earned."

"Yeah, yeah, I've heard that line before, sister," Manford complained. "Easy for you to say. You're beautiful and...normal. You don't look like a circus freak the world laughs at." Manford crawled to his feet and then kicked snow over toward the hunting knife. "Stupid knife...never should have tried that dumb thing."

Sarah touched Amanda's arm. "Go inside and order us

some coffee," she whispered through the wind. Amanda nodded her head and hurried inside. "Mr. Sappers—"

"Call me Manford," he said in a grumpy voice. "I ain't no mister. I'm just a...low-life thug who can't even rob two women without getting busted. My old lady must be laughing in her grave right now."

Sarah slowly placed her hands behind her back, studied the snow, the bare parking lot, and then turned her attention to the front of O'Mally's. "It's very warm inside...and nice."

"Yeah, I bet it is," Manford nodded his head. "Why don't I just waltz inside and go on a shopping spree?"

"We could go inside and get some coffee and food?"

Manford stared at Sarah. "Ain't you a cop?" he demanded as snow slapped at his wind-burned cheeks. "Cops ain't supposed to be nice to us criminals, remember? It's you against us, hot stuff. That's the rules."

"I'm a retired cop," Sarah calmly reminded Manford.

"Ain't no such thing," Manford said, lowered his head against a blast of icy wind, and sighed. "I knew Alaska was cold, but I didn't think it would be this cold...at least it'll be warm in jail."

"Why are you in Alaska?" Sarah asked Manford, keeping her voice calm.

"I wanted to build a snowman, okay?" Manford answered in his sarcastic voice.

"Okay, have it your way," Sarah told Manford. She nodded her head at the glass doors. "I'll be inside at the snack bar if you decide to come to your senses and stop acting like a jerk." Sarah turned and began to walk away.

"Hey...wait...I'm supposed to be going to jail...remember?" Manford called out in a frantic voice.

"So go turn yourself in," Sarah yelled over her shoulder and continued into O'Mally's.

"Go turn myself...in?" Manford asked in a confused voice. He threw his eyes down at the snow, spotted the hunting knife, and threw his hands up into the air. "Go turn myself in, she says?"

Sarah walked into a blast of warm air, turned left, and walked down a glossy hardwood floor in front of a row of four cash register stations that retained the same cozy, vintage, nineteen-fifties design as the day they'd been installed. An inviting snack bar nestled up in the far corner of the store, waiting for Sarah like a warm blanket next to a winter fireplace. The snack bar, like the cash registers, offered original white and red vinyl booths, a juke box, and checkered tiled floors, with old photos of actors hanging on the walls along with college pennants. "I love this place," Sarah smiled as she walked to the snack bar.

Amanda stood at the counter, taking in a deep breath of freshly brewed coffee and kosher chili dogs. Amy Huntsdale, a pretty twenty-one-year-old girl with long black hair, stared at Amanda with worried eyes. Whenever Amanda Hardcastle visited the snack bar, she usually gobbled up every hot dog in sight. Most customers went for a cheeseburger, but Amanda tore into the kosher chili dogs as if she were a starving wolf. Not that selling so much food was a bad thing, it was just that Mr. O'Mally was a bit on the cheap side and never ordered enough kosher hot dogs to last through the month —not as long as Amanda was in town. And when the snack bar ran low, Mr. O'Mally blamed Amy, for some reason. "What...will it be, Amanda?" Amy asked in a nervous voice, twirling a lock of her hair behind one ear.

"I think I'll start off with—" Amanda began to speak.

"Put your tongue back in your mouth, girl," Sarah interrupted and gently bumped Amanda's shoulder. "I don't think Mr. O'Mally's truck has come in yet, right Amy?"

"Not until the end of the month, I'm afraid," Amy nodded her head. "We're...still running a little low on kosher hot dogs."

Sarah smiled at Amy. Amy was such a pretty young woman; such lovely blue eyes and a smile that could melt an iceberg—when Amy smiled, that was. She could be a somber girl, a gray cloud on a sunny day, it seemed. Even the black and white waitress dress Mr. O'Mally required all snack bar employees to wear fit well with Amy's complexion. It broke Sarah's heart to see the young woman so nervous and beaten down by life. "How are you adapting to Snow Falls?" she asked.

"Better. I like it more than the town I came from in Maryland," Amy answered Sarah, then quickly dropped her eyes down to the red and chrome counter. "I like it here," she confessed. "It's very peaceful. I don't want to ever leave."

"I'm sure your mother is glad to have you living with her," Sarah assured Amy with a warm smile.

"You bet," Amanda beamed. "Mrs. Huntsdale has been crowing with joy all over town now that her baby girl is living here with her. Now, about those kosher chili dogs—"

"Not now," Sarah whispered and nudged Amanda with her elbow. "Look over there," she said and nodded toward the front entrance with her eyes.

Amanda turned toward the front entrance and spotted Manford looking around, lost and confused. "I thought you ran the little guy off," she whispered.

"He needs our help," Sarah whispered back. "Amy, honey, we need three large coffees and as many cheeseburgers as you can cook...and don't forget the fries."

Amy spotted Manford's messy hair and the threadbare clothing barely keeping him warm. Her heard broke. "Oh, he looks so...pitiful," she said in a sad voice.

"He's very hungry," Sarah whispered and quickly patted Amy's hand. "Get to work, honey," she pleaded. "And don't worry, I'm going to leave you a very nice tip."

"Oh, I don't need a tip. I—" Amy began to object.

"A nice tip, honey," Sarah smiled at Amy with caring eyes and then pulled Amanda over to a far booth and sat down. "Please don't give him a hard time," she begged.

Amanda tossed her purse down onto the seat, sat down next to Sarah, and watched Manford look in her direction and grinned. "Just a little teasing?"

Sarah set down her purse. "June Bug, you're impossible."

Amanda patted Sarah's hand. "I'll behave, love, I promise."

Manford spotted Sarah and Amanda, drew in a deep breath, and slowly walked toward the snack bar. When he reached the booth where Sarah and Amanda were sitting, he stopped. "If you're going to buy me food, I want to earn it. I decided that I'll do some chores for you. Deal?" he asked.

Sarah looked at Amanda. Amanda grinned. "Sounds good," Sarah told Manford and patted the table. "Sit down and take a load off. Coffee and food will be here in a few minutes." Manford glanced toward the snack bar counter, saw the pretty girl staring at him as she poured the coffee, and then he blushed and hurried into his seat.

Sarah watched Manford blow warm breath onto his bare, frozen hands. "You need a pair of winter gloves."

"I don't take charity," Manford said once again. "Listen...it's nice of you to overlook my...bad manners outside, okay, but don't think I'm going to let you baby me. I can tell. You think you're going to swaddle me up in baby clothes and stick a bottle in my mouth."

"I—" Sarah began.

"Yeah, yeah, I know," Manford told Sarah, hunching into himself, hunger still gnawing at him. "I'm a little person...I'm oh so cute, right? How adorable was it that a funny little person tried to rob you, right? Oh, you can't wait to tell all of your friends about me and laugh about how adorable it was to see the little person try to steal your purses while freezing his buns off." Manford rolled his eyes. "Everyone is the same...no one takes me seriously. Even when I was tossed in the jug for stealing, the cops treated me like I was some sideshow...and the inmates...I was a laughing stock to those guys."

"Mr. Sappers, I—" Sarah tried to object.

"My name is Manford, okay?" Manford insisted.

"Okay...Manford it is."

"Cut the act, cop, you think you're so polite—" Manford started to say.

"Why not call him a jerk?" Amanda asked calmly, interrupting him. "That's what he's acting like."

"Am not," Manford objected.

"Are too," Amanda fired at Manford, threw her foot under the table, and kicked his leg.

"Hey...why did you kick me?" Manford exclaimed in pain.

"Tall or short, doesn't matter to me," Amanda informed Manford. "Whenever a bloke is rude, I kick him."

Manford reached down and rubbed his leg. "I'm not rude."

"No? Could have fooled me. Sounds like you think it's okay to be rude since you're just feeling sorry for yourself for being short," Amanda told Manford.

"I don't feel sorry for myself, you...you English crumpet. I just hate it when people treat me like I'm some kind of circus freak," Manford snapped.

"Oh, go cry me a river," Amanda said and rolled her eyes.

"Well, you didn't seem very scared of me when I pulled

my knife out," Manford told Amanda. "I saw you. You nearly broke out laughing."

Amanda shrugged her shoulders. "It's not every day a child tries to rob me."

"See," Manford insisted. "I'm not a child, I'm a grown man."

"Are you? You don't act like one." Amanda rolled her eyes again. "You act like a little child."

"Making fun of my size...real mature."

"I'm making fun of how silly you looked shivering your tush off in the snow," Amanda told Manford.

"You did look silly," Sarah agreed. "Only a kid or a very, very foolish person would be out in that weather wearing such a thin jacket. It's hardly your size that's not intimidating, I'm afraid."

"Well, even if you dressed me in a three-piece suit, I still couldn't fix my height," Manford sighed. "That's my problem...always will be."

Sarah placed her hands together. "Manford, what are you doing in Snow Falls?" she asked. "Other than freezing your backside off, I mean."

Manford looked down at his thawing hands. "None of your business."

"Rude," Amanda said and kicked Manford's foot again.

"Hey...knock it off! Go have a tea party with the Queen or something."

Amanda kicked his foot twice. "I don't drink tea with the Queen, you smart-mouth little tosser."

Manford winced and rubbed his ankle where she had kicked him.

"Manford," Sarah said, keeping her voice easy, "it's not every day a stranger like yourself—"

"You mean a little person. A little person is the term if you don't want to be *rude*," he said to Sarah, aiming the last word over at Amanda with a brief glare.

Sarah nodded her head. "It's not every day a...a little person shows up in Snow Falls."

"Never mind one that tries to rob two women...dressed like a street bum who just arrived from somewhere much, much warmer," Amanda added.

Manford saw Amy walking over carrying three tall brown mugs on a tray. He quickly lowered his eyes to hide his eagerness.

"Here you are," Amy said, carefully placing the three mugs down onto the table. She added a bowl of creamers and sugar packets, and then looked at Sarah. "Your food will be out shortly. The grill was cold, so I had to warm it up first. Sorry."

"That's fine, honey." Sarah smiled at Amy.

Amy forced a nervous smile to her face, then, to Sarah and Amanda's surprise, the girl reached into her apron pocket, pulled out a candy bar, and placed it down next to Manford. "This should hold you over until the food is ready," she said, blushing, and hurried away.

Manford stared at the candy bar, then raised his eyes and watched Amy hurry back behind the counter and to the grill. "Now why did she do that?" he asked.

"Maybe Amy was being nice?" Sarah offered, clearly seeing that Manford wasn't used to kindness being offered to him.

"I don't need charity," Manford grumbled and pushed the candy bar away.

Amanda kicked his leg. "That wasn't charity, you bloke."

"Will you stop? My ankle is already frozen, and now it's going to turn black and blue," Manford begged.

"Then eat the candy bar," Amanda ordered.

Manford glanced at the candy bar and then drew in a deep breath of hot coffee steam. His mouth began to water. "Okay...since you insist," he said, snatched up the candy bar, and tore into it like a man who hadn't eaten in years, making Sarah wonder how long it had been since Manford had eaten a decent meal.

"Manford—" Sarah began to ask.

Manford raised his left hand. "No personal questions, hot stuff," he said, scarfing down the chocolate in four quick bites. "My personal life is my business...and you," he said, pointed at Amanda, tucked his legs back, and shook his head, "can't kick the answers out of me, okay?"

Sarah shook her head. Manford sure was going to be a hard case to solve. But, she thought, and glanced toward the front entrance and studied the snow storm outside, maybe the weather might help her. She was certain Manford didn't have a place to stay and was most likely sleeping in vacant rental cabins and foraging around for food. A hot meal, a warm bath, and a soft bed might encourage the little guy to loosen his tongue. "I just wanted to know where you were going to spend the night?" she asked. "We can give you a ride there." She knew he didn't have a place to go but was hoping this would at least start to build trust.

Amanda looked at Sarah and rolled her eyes. "Mittens wasn't enough, love?"

"I don't need mittens. Or gloves," Manford said. He grabbed his coffee and began chugging it down without adding any creamer or sugar. The hot coffee mug began defrosting his hands and his insides.

"No, Mittens is my dog," Sarah explained, slowly took

her own coffee, added one sugar and one creamer, stirred it with a spoon, and took a sip. "Not bad."

Amanda prepared her coffee. "Mittens is a Siberian Husky," she told Manford. "She's a good dog."

"I don't like dogs and dogs don't like me," Manford grumbled, speaking a clear lie into the air. The truth was Manford loved dogs and dogs loved him. As a small boy he once owned a German Shepherd named Shep who he loved with all of his heart. Shep had been his very best friend, until...

"Manford?" Sarah asked, seeing Manford's eyes drift off into a painful memory.

"Huh...what?" Manford asked. He shook his head, looked down at his coffee, and took a sip. "I...uh...I have a place to sleep," he said, answering Sarah's question. "I don't need a ride."

Amanda glanced at Sarah. "Sure," she said in a doubtful voice.

"The knife you pulled on us," Sarah told Manford, "had a broken tip...like maybe it got broken trying to pry open a locked door?"

Manford gulped. "I...don't know what you're talking about."

"I'm sure if I had my dear husband go check on the rental cabins in the area—just in case a vagrant wanted on assault with a deadly weapon might be hiding there—he might find one or two cabins that have been broken into," Sarah explained. "Of course," she added, "I don't see why a person would break into a rental cabin. Andrew, the Chief of Police, started requiring that all the power to rental cabins be cut after we had...a few problems with some bad people hiding out in them."

"Bad people...hah," Amanda said. "Deadly killers is more like it."

"Drink your coffee, honey," Sarah begged Amanda.

"Deadly killers?" Manford asked. He felt his face turn pale. "What do you mean...deadly killers? Way out here in the middle of nowhere?"

"Go to the library and go through the newspapers and you'll read all about who has visited our cozy, quiet little town," Amanda promised Manford. She took a sip of her coffee, looked around, and continued. "I would stay out of those rental cabins if I were you," she said, deliberately setting a trap for Manford.

"I ain't afraid of no one...I've been perfectly safe in mine, so—" Manford stopped talking and realized he had let his pride cause him to fall into a hole.

"In your cabin?" Sarah asked.

Manford dropped his eyes, stared at his coffee, and gave up. "Okay, okay...so I broke into an empty cabin. What do you expect a guy to do...freeze to death? It ain't like someone was using the cabin anyway."

"Breaking and entering is against the law," Sarah pointed out. "The owner of the cabin you're staying at might not appreciate you breaking the law."

"Listen, hot stuff, it's either break the law or freeze to death."

Sarah took a sip of her coffee. "How about we compromise?" she asked.

"Compromise?"

"I won't turn you in for breaking and entering, or the armed robbery attempt, for that matter...if you stay at my cabin," Sarah explained.

Manford stared at Sarah. "Are you for real?" he asked. "Why, I could rob you blind in no time—"

"And go where with your armful of loot?" Sarah called Manford's bluff. "Manford, there's a snow storm kicking around outside that's growing worse by the hour. I don't want your death on my conscience, but I also can't just let you walk out of here and break into someone's cabin."

"The snow storm isn't too bad right now. Plows are keeping the streets clear," Amanda explained. "To an outsider, the storm might seem bad already, but for us northerners, the weather is simply being fussy right now.

But by tonight, everyone with good sense will be indoors cuddled up around a hot fire."

Manford studied his coffee. As he did, Amy hurried over with a plate of two cheeseburgers heaped with fries and one long pickle. She set the plate down in front of Manford. "I'll be back with more," she promised and whisked away like a gust of wind.

The aroma of the two delicious cheeseburgers crawled down Manford's hungry throat. He let go of his coffee, and without being able to control himself, grabbed a cheeseburger and gobbled it down in five bites. The second cheeseburger didn't go any slower. "Good," he said, wiping his mouth with the arm of the worn-down coat he was wearing. He started in on the fries, licking salt from his fingertips.

Sarah began to speak but stopped when she spotted Conrad stepping through the front entrance. Conrad looked around and then focused his attention on the snack bar, saw Sarah, and waved his right hand at her over the racks of clothing and other displays. Sarah stood up. "Uh...excuse me, Manford. My husband is here. Don't worry...I don't think this is about you..."

Amanda turned and saw Conrad waving at Sarah. The expression on his face sent a cold chill down her spine. "Oh no, he's wearing one of those faces..." she moaned.

Sarah excused herself and hurried to Conrad. "What's

wrong, honey?" she asked.

Conrad kept his eyes on the snack bar. "Who is that sitting with Amanda?" he asked, shaking snow off his leather jacket.

"Manford Sappers," Sarah explained as Manford began shifting back and forth in the booth, keeping his eyes ducked low.

Conrad stopped shaking snow off his jacket. "Sarah, honey," he said in a low voice, "I...maybe we better talk privately?" he said, spotting Amanda staring at him with worried eyes.

Sarah followed Conrad out into the little vestibule between the inner and outer doors of the department store. "What is it?" she asked, feeling the icy winds seep through the outer doors and chill her face.

Conrad looked around. All he spotted was white snow covering the few trucks in the otherwise bare parking lot. "Sarah, Mrs. Appleson was found dead a couple of hours ago."

"Mrs. Appleson...doesn't she own the candle shop?" Sarah asked.

Conrad nodded his head. "Sarah, the woman was strangled to death," he explained. "Macy Appleson found the body."

"Macy Appleson?"

"Mrs. Appleson's daughter," Conrad explained. "Mrs. Appleson was found lying in her backyard near a woodpile."

Sarah stood in shock. "Conrad—you don't think..." she stopped, her face drained of color. "I didn't even know her that well..."

"I know what you're thinking, honey," Conrad said in a quick voice. "You're wondering if Mrs. Appleson's murder is connected to your old life somehow. That's why I found you as soon as I was able to get away from the station." Conrad studied the snow. "Sarah, how well did you know Mrs. Appleson?"

Sarah stared into her husband's eyes. "I didn't know her well at all," she confessed. "Mrs. Appleson was never a friendly lady. I visited her candle shop maybe...two times at the most. I only remember her name because Amanda made a joke about her one time...something about how Mrs. Appleson would make a sour pie...something along that line. At the time Amanda's joke struck me as funny, so I always remembered it whenever I heard her name..."

Conrad bit down on his lip. "Macy Appleson swears that her mother didn't have any enemies," he told Sarah, allowing a gust of icy wind to rush over his face. The cold helped him focus. "I'm not so sure about Macy Appleson, though."

"I've never met Macy Appleson."

"Not a lot of people have," Conrad explained. "Macy Appleson is an actress—not a very successful one, apparently—who has been staying with her mother for the last couple of months." Conrad looked around through the outer doors. The snow, as beautiful as it was, was tainted with ugly murder once again. "Macy claims she needed time away from Los Angeles...time to 'find herself'."

"I'm sure we'll find out more about her when you run her background."

"I can't," Conrad complained. "The entire system at the station house is still down."

"Still?" Sarah asked. "I thought Andrew said the system would be up and running today?"

Conrad shook his head. "System is down all over the state," he explained. "Whoever hacked into the system and shut it down sure knew what they were doing. All priority emergency cases are being coordinated with outside agencies by phone until the system is up and running again. Small-time stuff—"

"Mrs. Appleson isn't small-time stuff, honey. You said she was strangled to death."

"Yeah, she was. But you know the deal, Sarah. First we have to send the body off and have an autopsy done, and then we have to wait for the report." Conrad shook his head. "With the system down and the network frazzled, there's no way our case will be put on the front burner."

Sarah understood Conrad's frustration. "Honey, I...I can talk with Macy."

"I think you should," Conrad agreed in a worried voice. "Macy is from the Los Angeles area."

Sarah stared into Conrad's eyes as her mind frantically searched through the memory files locked away in a protected room in her mind that she tried not to venture into often. "I...honey, her name just doesn't ring a bell."

Conrad reached out and put a loving hand on his wife's shoulder. "Sarah, someone murdered Mrs. Appleson and that someone is still loose." Conrad looked at the inner doors. "Speaking of someone being on the loose, who is this guy you found?"

Sarah sighed. "Manford Sappers. He tried to rob me earlier," she told Conrad and then explained all about Manford as the wind and snow listened with curious ears. When Sarah finished speaking, Conrad slowly pulled out a pair of handcuffs. "I know what you have to do."

"I wish I didn't," Conrad promised and walked Sarah back inside the warm department store.

Far away, the real killer sat next to a warm fire, sipping a hot cup of tea.

CHAPTER TWO

Manford gave Sarah a look that said it all. "You cops are all the same," he groused, walked over to a bumpy cot, and plopped down like an angry rag doll. "Sure...feed the little person before you throw him in the jug."

Sarah sighed. "Manford, a woman is dead," she said and placed her right hand against the bars covering the cell door Manford was locked behind. "You tried to rob me and Amanda at knifepoint. You're a stranger in town and you won't tell us why you're here. And," she added, "you admitted to breaking into a vacant rental cabin. So, what is my husband supposed to think?"

Manford felt Sarah's words strike him in the face like a hard hand hitting him over and over. "Yeah...yeah...I guess I do look guilty," he confessed and forced his anger into a corner. "I guess if I was the fuzz, I would lock me up, too."

Sarah stared at Manford. The poor guy looked like he was at the end of his rope. At least, she thought, he had two cheeseburgers and some coffee in his stomach. "Amanda is buying you some proper winter clothes," she said, hoping to make Manford feel better.

"Yeah...I guess she's a nice gal," Manford said and dared to look up at Sarah. To his surprise, he saw a very caring woman instead of a cruel, heartless cop. "I didn't kill nobody," he told Sarah in a serious voice. "I ain't no killer."

"I believe you," Sarah promised Manford.

Manford studied Sarah's eyes. The one true skill he had was reading people's eyes—the one true skill he relied on to get by. It was clear that Sarah was speaking the truth. "Why do you believe me? Because you think I'm too short to kill someone?"

Sarah sighed and nodded her head yes. "Mrs. Appleson was a tall woman...five foot eleven inches, I believe. She was strangled to death. Someone surprised her." Sarah removed her hand from the jail cell door. "Manford, cop or no cop, simple math indicates that the woman was likely strangled by a person taller than you."

"I could have used a chair."

"Nope," Sarah shook her head. "Not in this blowing snow. Not without her seeing you."

Manford frowned. "I could have used a ladder."

"Nope," Sarah shook her head again.

"I could have...jumped up on her back, knocked her over," Manford insisted, defending his height. Being told that he couldn't be a killer because of his height made him feel defensive. Sure, he wasn't a killer, but being told it was because of his height rather than his morals was...painful.

"Manford, my husband showed me photos of the crime scene. Whoever killed Mrs. Appleson swept away all the tracks in the snow, so we don't know the killer's shoe size. However, according to the trail the killer left—"

"With the branch?"

Sarah nodded her head. "The killer swept a clean trail all the way to the northeast side of the property, where the tracks were lost. The rental cabin you broke into—yes, we did find it—is located at the southwest end of the county. Besides that," Sarah added, "Mrs. Appleson's cabin is at least a half hour's walk from O'Mally's—"

"I could have killed the woman and high-tailed it to the store," Manford insisted.

"Not through the woods," Sarah continued in a patient

voice. "Mrs. Appleson's cabin is located on a road by several other cabins."

"So?"

"So the plows are running," Sarah explained patiently. "Plus, people are out and about. Someone would have seen you, Manford, if you walked to O'Mally's using the streets, or high-tailed it, or whatever."

"I could have gone through the woods."

Sarah shook her head. "You're not an outdoors person, Manford. Not in those clothes, anyway. There's no way you could have navigated these woods and found your way to O'Mally's."

"I could—"

"You could have showed up at Mrs. Appleson's on foot before dawn, hidden yourself behind the wood pile, and jumped on her back? You could have walked to Mrs. Appleson's without being seen? You could have dodged the plows? You could have done a lot of things, Manford, but what you didn't do was kill Mrs. Appleson," Sarah said in a voice that told Manford to stop playing tough. "You don't know this area, Manford. You're a stranger in a rural Alaskan town who can barely find his way from point A to point B."

Manford didn't like Sarah throwing the truth in his face, but, he admitted, the truth was...well, the truth. "Okay, yeah, I can find my way around a big city a lot better than I can the woods...good enough? Satisfied? Manford is a useless city boy, okay?"

Sarah sighed. "Manford, I didn't say that. You're not a useless city boy."

"Sure I am," Manford insisted. "I tried to make it seem like I could be the killer and you used my inexperience to knock me down into the snow."

"All I did was throw a lot of assumptions in the air and let you take the bait," Sarah explained. "Manford, I know you didn't kill Mrs. Appleson."

"Your husband doesn't seem to agree."

Sarah looked down the short hallway leading away from the holding cells. "Conrad is worried that you might have arrived in town with another person. His thinking is very practical, Manford. You can't blame him for being suspicious of you. After all, you did pull a knife on his wife."

"Yeah, yeah," Manford rolled his eyes, "you're constantly reminding me of that."

Sarah focused back on Manford. "You know, I was supposed to be in London right now with Amanda. I owe her a trip. Instead we decided to postpone the trip...well, Amanda decided to postpone the trip...because her son came for a lovely visit last week."

"How nice," Manford rolled his eyes.

"My point is," Sarah continued, ignoring Manford's sarcasm, "is that you should be glad I didn't go to London. Right now, Amanda and I are the only friends you have in town."

"I don't need no friends."

Sarah shook her head. "Why are you so stubborn?" she demanded. "I'm trying to help you."

"You feel sorry for me. There's a difference, hot stuff."

Sarah stared at Manford. The truth was...the man was right. "Okay, so I feel sorry for you. Is that a crime?"

"I don't need pity...don't you understand a man has his pride?" Manford snapped and flung his arms together.

"Pride before goeth destruction," Sarah said, quoting the Bible.

"Yeah...my mother used to tell me the same Bible verse," Manford told Sarah. "She used to tell me my anger just fueled my pride...guess she was right."

Sarah leaned against the jail cell door. "Manford," she said in a tired voice, "what are you doing in Snow Falls? Let me help you, please."

Manford lowered his eyes. "My business is my business, okay?"

"No, it's not okay, because a woman is dead, and a town wants answers. You want a whole bunch of angry people forming a lynch mob?"

"So let 'em," Manford grumbled. "They'll sure get a laugh out of seeing a little person hanging from a rope, kicking his short legs in midair."

Sarah closed her eyes. "You're obstinate, I give you that," she told Manford.

"I run solo," Manford replied. "In this life, hot stuff, the only person you can trust is yourself. My old man taught me that after he betrayed..." Manford caught his mouth.

Sarah opened her eyes, looked at Manford, saw him staring down at his hands, and decided not to push any more. "Okay, Manford, I'll leave you alone for now and give you time to think."

"Thanks."

"Want a cup of coffee before I go?" Sarah asked.

Manford shrugged his shoulders. "I don't care."

Sarah felt like rushing into the cell, grabbing Manford into her arms, and hugging the spite right out of him. He was like a stubborn little brother. "I'll go get you a cup of coffee," she said in a caring voice and walked to the coffee station. Conrad and Andrew were standing at the coffee station talking. "Any news?" she asked.

Conrad shook his head. "System is still down," he said and nodded his head back toward the holding area. "Anything?"

Sarah shook her head. "Manford is a tough cookie," she explained and then added: "But he's no killer, Conrad."

Andrew took a sip of hot coffee. "He could be, Sarah. Why else won't he tell us his business? After all this town has been through, I wouldn't be surprised one little bit."

Conrad studied his wife's beautiful face. "Any idea why Manford came to Snow Falls?" he asked.

"No," Sarah sighed, picked up a brown coffee cup, and filled it with hot coffee. "My guess is he's running from someone and tried to get as far away as possible."

"Like maybe the person who killed Mrs. Appleson?" Conrad asked, hoping his wife's brilliant mind would shed some light on his murder case. To his disappointment, Sarah shook her head no. "No?"

"No," Sarah confirmed. "The murder of Mrs. Appleson is not connected to Manford in any way, shape, fashion or form...or to myself, for that matter."

"How can you be so sure, Sarah?" Andrew asked.

Sarah studied the coffee creamer can and a white sugar shaker on the coffee station table. "My gut," she finally spoke. "Andrew, my gut is telling me that the murder of Mrs. Appleson was carried out by someone who maybe at best knows my name." Sarah looked at Conrad with eyes that held relief and sadness. "Find that woman's killer, honey. I'll handle Manford."

Conrad nodded his head. "Deal," he said, studying Sarah's eyes. "You're really concerned about Manford, aren't you?"

"Manford needs a lot of love and care," Sarah explained. "I don't think he's trusted anyone in a long, long time. He needs some good old-fashioned hospitality and friendship. And speaking of..." she said and turned to Andrew, "maybe you can release him into my custody?"

"Hey, wait a minute," Andrew objected. "I'm wearing my Chief of Police uniform, Sarah. I can't go breaking the law. No ma'am...no way...sorry."

"I understand," Sarah assured Andrew and then, to Conrad's shock, she let a tear fall from her eye. "It's just that...Manford isn't safe here. He needs love...someone to care for him...to steer him onto the right path...oh, it's all so sad."

"Hey...Sarah...oh, no...she's crying," Andrew moaned. He quickly set down his coffee and waved a shaky hand in the air. "Now, don't cry...don't cry..."

Conrad turned his head and grinned, watching his friend attempt to get out of this situation.

"I...well, it's just that you see, Manford is a suspect in a certain case—"

"A murder case!" Sarah whispered and then broke out into a miserable sob.

"Oh, not that...please, anything but that..." Andrew looked to Conrad for help. Conrad shrugged his shoulders. "It's just that...Sarah, you even told us Manford Sappers pulled a knife on you and Amanda—"

"But he's so sorry," Sarah cried and flung her face into Conrad's shoulder. "He didn't mean it! He was just starving and freezing to death! Oh, the poor man..."

Andrew shook a nervous hand at Sarah. "I didn't mean to make you cry...I...well, I'm a cop, Sarah...we're all cops...we know the rules and..." Andrew stopped babbling and listened to Sarah cry. His face twisted into a painful knot. "Oh...I...well, how far could a little man like that get in this weather?" he muttered to himself. "I suppose it wouldn't harm anybody if he was released..."

Sarah lifted her head and looked at Andrew with tear-filled eyes. "I promise to watch him like a hawk and take full responsibility for him. I'll place him under house arrest in my cabin and keep him there. I promise."

Andrew sighed. "Well...the system is down...and I haven't taken an official report from you or Amanda yet...and there isn't no proof that Manford Sappers killed Mrs. Appleson..." Andrew ran his hands through his red hair. "Okay, Sarah, I'm going to release Manford Sappers into your custody...just for the time being, though, until we find out who really killed Mrs. Appleson and clear Sappers of any suspicion."

Sarah wiped her tears away. Her smile came back quickly. "Thank you, Chief," she smiled, knowing that being called by his official title always made Andrew feel good inside his heart.

"You just be careful of that little guy," Andrew warned Sarah in a tough, fatherly voice. "Detective," he told Conrad, "release the prisoner into Mrs. Spencer's custody."

"Yes sir, Chief" Conrad told Andrew and smiled as Andrew marched away to his office like a proud rooster who hadn't just been henpecked out of the barn yard.

Sarah hugged Conrad's arm. "Did I overdo it with the waterworks?" she whispered.

"A little," Conrad grinned and then grew serious. "I hope you know what you're doing, Sarah. Manford Sappers isn't as innocent as he looks. Just because he's short doesn't mean he isn't deadly."

"Manford isn't a killer," Sarah promised Conrad.

"He pulled a knife on you."

"A rusted hunting knife with a broken tip," Sarah counteracted.

"A weapon is a weapon," Conrad pointed out. "Keep your gun in your holster or locked in the safe at all times."

Sarah nodded her head. "Of course."

Conrad pointed to the holding area. "Sarah, this town has seen a lot of murder committed by some very deadly people who gave us a run for our money." Conrad picked up his coffee mug and took a sip of coffee. "We're not invincible, honey. We're human before we're cops. Just remember that."

Sarah loved Conrad for worrying over her. "Manford would never hurt me. At best he might try to steal my purse and run. And how far could he get?"

"Now, why doesn't that make me feel any better?" Conrad asked Sarah in a miserable voice.

Sarah understood her husband's concern. "I need to find out who Manford is, why he's in town, and who he's running from. This is the only way."

"If Manford is running from someone," Conrad said, "the person he's running from might end up right here in Snow Falls. That person might follow him right to our cabin."

"I've thought of that," Sarah assured Conrad.

Conrad bit down on his lower lip. "Sarah, honey, are you sure Manford isn't involved with the murder of Mrs. Appleson?"

"I'm sure," Sarah replied and patted Conrad's arm. "Manford isn't connected to the murder."

"How can you be so sure?" Conrad asked.

"Because I've studied his eyes," Sarah explained. "Conrad, Manford is running from danger...he's not looking for trouble."

Conrad looked into Sarah's eyes for a long time. "I've learned to trust you with my life," he smiled. "If you think Manford is connected to some other trouble, well then, I believe you," he said and gently kissed Sarah. "If a husband can't trust his wife, he's not much good. Now, let's go get your new house guest out of his holding cell."

Sarah smiled into Conrad's eyes. "I promise to be very careful and if anything starts to go wrong, I will let you know immediately."

"I know you will, honey," Conrad told Sarah, softly kissed her again, and then made his way toward the holding cell where a very depressed Manford was waiting.

Manford climbed out of the front seat of Sarah's jeep, looked up into a dark, gray sky dripping with heavy snow, and then focused on the warm cabin in front of him. The sight of the warm cabin created images of raging fireplaces, hot mugs of cocoa, toasty blankets, cozy beds, and—yes—hot showers. The cabin he had broken into had not only lacked power but also hot water. "Nice place," he told Sarah.

Sarah walked around the front of her jeep. "It's small but cozy," she said as a large, wet snowflake landed on her nose. She wiped the snowflake away and glanced toward the front yard. In her mind, she saw a creepy snowman gnawing a candy cane and wearing a leather jacket—the same old sinister vision that haunted her every time a deadly crime came to town. The snowman grinned at her but said nothing. "Let's get inside, okay? I need to check on Mittens."

Manford hesitated. He looked up at Sarah with uneasy eyes. "I don't need charity," he insisted. "I can...run any second I want."

"Sure, you can," Sarah said and looked up at the sky. "But it'll be dark soon and you wouldn't get far. But if you want to freeze to death, I suppose that's your choice." Sarah lowered her hand and made her way through the snow toward the backdoor. "I'm going inside to make a pot of coffee and cook us something to eat," she called out.

Manford stood still for a few seconds and watched Sarah walk away through snow and icy winds, feeling his feet quickly turning into blocks of ice. He had only just recently warmed up, sitting in the holding cell, and the idea of staying outside any longer ripped at his will and instinct to run. "I'll play this game for what it's worth and split...yeah, that's what I'll do," he said in an uneasy voice and quickly hurried after Sarah.

Sarah unlocked the back door to the cabin, walked into the kitchen, and spotted Mittens lying in her doggy bed. "Hello girl, how are you?"

Mittens let out a happy little whine and thumped her tail against the bed eagerly. She raised her right front leg. The leg was wrapped in a sterile bandage. When Manford appeared in the doorway she lowered her front leg and, to Sarah's surprise, began wagging her tail even faster. Manford saw Mittens and almost smiled. Instead, he bit down hard on his lip and forced himself to look away. "That dog better not bite me."

Sarah glanced at Manford. "Mittens never bites," she said and closed the back door. "Amanda will be over soon with your clothes. She'll be spending the night with us."

"Hey, you didn't mention that," Manford objected.

"I'm sorry, do I need to run my plans by you?" She gave him a look and he looked down, shame faced. "Amanda's husband is still in London," Sarah explained and began removing her coat. "Amanda stays over a lot when her husband is out of town."

Manford watched Sarah hang her coat up on a wooden coat rack next to the back door. Underneath the coat he saw a thick, warm, gray and white dress that reminded him of something a granny might wear. Yet, he noticed, Sarah wore the dress with a special beauty...a motherly beauty rather than a romantic beauty; the kind of a beauty his own mother once had. "Nice dress."

Sarah smiled. "Thank you," she replied. "This dress was a gift from a dear friend of mine who lives in Los Angeles. He bought me this dress because it reminded him of the dress I was wearing the first time we met."

"An old boyfriend, huh?" Manford asked, allowing the warm heat of the kitchen to soak into his body.

Sarah let out a loud laugh. "Pete?" she asked. "Oh goodness no. Pete is like a father to me. Or an uncle, maybe." Sarah shook her head. "I can't wait to tell Pete you thought he was an old boyfriend. Oh, is he ever going to get a laugh."

"Yeah...that's me...good for laughs," Manford sighed.

"Oh, I didn't mean it that way, Manford," Sarah said and gently touched Manford's right arm. "If you knew Pete, you would understand. Now, let's not get in a dreary mood, okay? I'll make us a pot of coffee and then...oh, what do you say I make us some sandwiches?"

Manford shrugged his shoulders. "Your call."

"Coffee and sandwiches it is," Sarah smiled and pointed at Mittens. "But first Mittens needs her medicine." Sarah walked over to the kitchen counter and picked up a brown pill bottle. "I have to give Mittens a pill."

Manford looked at Mittens. As soon as he did, the dog began wagging her tail again. "How did...how did the mutt hurt herself?" he asked, struggling to sound tough.

"Part of a dead pine tree fell in the backyard while she was peeing out near the woods," Sarah explained as she removed the cap from the medicine bottle. "She darted away, but one of the limbs struck Mittens in her front leg." Sarah placed the lid down on the kitchen counter. "The winds were very strong the night she hurt herself and it was very dark."

Manford watched Mittens continue to wag her tail. He wanted to rush to the dog, check her hurt leg, and promise that everything was going to be alright. Preferably while petting the husky's ears, which looked soft as velvet. Instead, he stood very still and watched Sarah take the dog a large white pill. Mittens spotted the pill, stopped wagging her tail, and began to whine. "The mutt doesn't like the pill."

"Nope," Sarah said in a worried voice. She bent down and began petting Mittens' head. "But Dr. Branton has instructed me to give her this pill four times a day." Sarah lowered her head and kissed Mittens on the head. "Okay, girl, it's time." Mittens let out a low whine and tucked her good paw over her nose. "Oh, come on," Sarah pleaded, "it's not that bad." Mittens didn't agree. She kept her paw over her nose.

Manford shook his head. "You're never going to get that mutt to take her pill that way," he warned Sarah.

"Tell me about it," Sarah said. "Each time I have to force it down her throat."

"That's no good," Manford objected. He quickly ripped off the worn down coat he was wearing, slapped it onto the coat rack, and hurried over to Sarah. "Got any peanut butter?"

"Why...yes, I do. Why?" Sarah asked.

Manford brushed at a dirty green sweater covering his body, pulling up his sleeves. "Go get me some, huh?"

"Okay." Sarah hurried away to the refrigerator, opened it, brought out a jar of peanut butter, and walked back to Manford. Manford took the pill and the peanut butter. "What now?"

"Watch," Manford told Sarah. He opened the peanut butter jar, handed the lid to Sarah, and then dipped the pill in the peanut butter. "Now listen," he told Mittens, his voice going softer despite himself, "this here is some good stuff. It'll take away the nasty taste of the pill, so you stop fussing and be good."

Mittens looked up into Manford's eyes, saw a sweet heart staring down at her, and decided to mind. She lowered her paw. "Good girl." Manford actually smiled and, with a tender hand full of love and concern, slid the pill into the dog's mouth. Mittens quickly tasted the peanut butter, found it to be good, and then began chewing. When her taste buds encountered the sourness of the pill, she quickly swallowed and then turned her head to a silver water dish and began gulping down water. "The peanut butter will make her lick the inside of her mouth and pick up any residue left by the pill," Manford explained.

"Smart."

"My mom taught me that trick," Manford told Sarah. He reached out his hand and patted Mittens' head. "You're a pretty mutt...uh...dog."

Sarah smiled. "I'll make us a pot of coffee."

Manford glanced over his shoulder, saw Sarah walking away, and returned his attention back to Mittens. Mittens stopped drinking her water, looked up at Manford, and wagged her tail. "Yeah, you're okay, too," he smiled and then hurried to the kitchen table and sat down on a chair. "Nice kitchen."

"Small but cozy," Sarah said, filling a coffee pot full of water.

Manford gazed around the kitchen. The kitchen was cozy, warm and safe—blessedly safe. But even though the kitchen felt safe...his heart did not. "Uh...what do you do for a living?" he asked. "Besides being a retired cop?"

"I'm a writer," Sarah explained as she continued to work on making the coffee. A minute later, the smell of fresh coffee began to fill the air.

"What do you write?" Manford asked, not really caring, but wanting to make conversation.

"Crime books," Sarah told Manford in a voice that wandered through the air on troubled legs. "I write...crime books," she said again and made a path toward the refrigerator. "Okay, I've got turkey and roast beef. What will it be?"

"Turkey...with cheese, if you have any. But none of that awful mayonnaise. I eat my sandwiches plain," Manford told Sarah.

"I don't like mayonnaise, either," Sarah smiled. "But I do like cheese, tomato and lettuce along with barbeque chips."

Manford's mouth watered. He loved barbeque chips. "Sounds good."

Sarah smiled again, pulled out a bag of deli turkey meat, a tray of cheese, a tomato, some lettuce, and a coconut cake. When Manford saw the coconut cake, his eyes grew wide. "Eat all the cake you want...after you eat your sandwich," Sarah told Manford and tossed him a wink.

Manford put his chin down on his hands and watched Sarah float around the kitchen fixing sandwiches, pouring coffee, and slicing cake. Sarah was so beautiful in his eyes. He felt as if he could melt in place. But, Manford told himself, Sarah's beauty wasn't a romantic beauty...it was a real, honest to goodness, motherly charm in his eyes. Sure, when he first saw Sarah he thought the woman was hot stuff, but the more he looked into her eyes, studied her face, he saw her beauty transform into something deep and personal—the kind of trustful person he hadn't met in a long, long time.

"Here you go," Sarah said, setting down a brown plate holding three large turkey sandwiches in front of Manford. She hurried away and returned with a bowl of chips and a mug full of hot coffee.

Manford waited for Sarah to bring her food to the table. "Uh...thanks," he said trying to sound somewhat polite.

Sarah smiled, bowed her head, prayed, and then said: "Amen."

"Uh...Amen," Manford whispered. He lowered his eyes down to his food and sighed. "Thanks...for the food...Lord," he whispered again and then picked up one of the sandwiches and took a bite. "Not bad...what is that...pepper jack cheese?"

Sarah nodded her head. "I love pepper jack cheese."

"Me, too," Manford admitted, smiling at her shyly

49

without knowing or understanding why. Maybe because he was warm, safe, and being fed. Maybe because he wasn't cold, hungry or alone, or facing the prospect of sleeping another night in a dark and friendless place, terrified at every sound. He took another bite of his sandwich and then took a sip of coffee. "I like my coffee black," he said, trying to sound tough.

"Me, too, at times," Sarah explained, taking a bite of her own sandwich. "At other times I like a little cream and sugar. It depends on my mood."

A strange feeling washed over Manford. He suddenly felt...what was the feeling...relaxed? Yes, he felt relaxed; the feeling was strange and alien. "I guess that makes sense," he said and took another bite of his sandwich. His eyes fell to the coconut cake resting on the kitchen counter. "Did you mean it when you said I can have as much as I want?"

"I sure did," Sarah smiled, noticing Manford's tense mood slowly dropping away. "And after you eat, I thought, if you want, you could go take a nice hot shower or have a hot bath? Whichever you want. Amanda should be here by then."

Manford chewed on his food. The sound of a hot shower sure was nice. "I might run out all the hot water. I ain't...had a hot shower...in a while."

"Don't worry about the hot water," Sarah smiled and then

lowered her voice into a secretive whisper: "Just between us, Amanda runs out all the hot water, too."

Manford looked into Sarah's warm eyes. "That friend of yours is really something special to you, huh?"

"Amanda has saved my life many times," Sarah told Manford. "She's not just my friend...she's a very special heartbeat inside of my soul."

"Must be nice to have a...to have..." Manford stumbled over his words. "To have...that," he finished. "A real friend, I mean."

"You don't have many of those?" Sarah asked carefully.

"What do you think?" Manford retorted. His voice softened a little as he continued, "And before you go asking about family...forget about it. My old man is dead and so is my mom." Manford put down his sandwich and lowered his eyes.

"I'm sorry," Sarah told Manford. "But please, don't stop eating. I know you're hungry."

Manford studied his sandwich and decided being depressed wasn't worth causing his stomach to remain hungry. "Yeah, I guess," he said and began working on his sandwich again.

Sarah picked up a chip and ate it. "We won't talk about friends or family, okay?"

"Thanks."

Sarah wiped her fingers and looked over at him, gauging. "The clothes Amanda bought you might not be a perfect fit," she said, changing the subject. "You might have to make do with a size too big. I hope that's okay."

"Does this sweater I'm wearing look like it fits me?" Manford asked. "This thing is like a dress on me." He cracked a half smile, gesturing to the unraveling ends of the sweater that trailed at the hem and the cuffs. It looked as if part of it had been cut off to make it shorter.

Sarah wondered again how he had managed to get all the way to Snow Falls. No bus stopped nearby, and there were very few roads that passed through going anywhere. It was clear that his journey had been very difficult and tiring. "Do you want me to throw those clothes away or wash them for you?"

Manford looked at Sarah and then glanced down at his dirty clothes. "These clothes remind me of who I am...where I came from. You best wash them for me."

Sarah felt her heart break. "Manford, you don't...I mean..." she stopped talking and looked down at her coffee. "I'll wash your clothes," she promised.

"Hey, don't be sad for me," Manford told Sarah. "These clothes just remind me that I'm a bum...a no-good bum that ain't gonna amount to nothing. Best to know who you are in life. Don't go getting notions above your station.

That's what my old man always told me as he dragged me and my mother around from town to town in that dirty..." Manford clamped down on his tongue. "Forget about it."

Sarah heard anger and pain grip Manford's voice. But what could she do? What could she say to a bitter man who was running not only from a physical danger, it seemed, but from an inner darkness from his past that threatened to tear his life and heart in two? So she said nothing. Instead, she let Manford eat in silence and listened to the snow storm howl and cry outside, wondering what in the world she was going to do with Manford Sappers when the storm was all over.

Manford Sappers was wondering the very same thing as he finished his sandwich, cursing his talkative tongue. He gazed longingly again at the coconut cake and decided that perhaps he better not have any. It would taste too good and he'd regret it when he left. It would just make him hungrier later when he had no food once again.

Far away, the killer who was chasing Manford was wondering just where his little friend was hiding. "I'll find you, Manford," a voice filled with greed and anger hissed, "and when I do, you're dead."

CHAPTER THREE

Manford slipped on a very warm white robe that almost swallowed his body whole. "Who cares," Manford said, standing in a steam-filled bathroom that smelled of fresh soap mixed with a fruity shampoo. "I'm warm, full and safe...for now," he finished and wiped steam off of an oval bathroom mirror that was unbearably girly, to his mind. He saw his reflection appear before the steam charged forward and recaptured the mirror. "I may be clean...but I'm still the same old Manford," he sighed, lowered his eyes, and shook his head.

"Manford?" Sarah called out from the hallway holding a bag full of newly bought clothes.

Manford sighed. "Yeah?" he called out.

"Amanda is here. She brought your clothes. I'm going to

leave them outside the bathroom door, okay?" Sarah explained, feeling like a mother rather than a friend. "She bought you some socks and...uh...underwear." Sarah felt her cheeks turn red. "There's a pair of brand new boots waiting for you in the kitchen," she added in a quick voice.

"Uh...yeah...okay," Manford called back. "Um...thanks. Just leave the bag outside the door, okay?"

Sarah set down a red and white striped bag that reminded her of a candy cane and, hearing nothing more from behind the door, walked back to the kitchen.

"Well?" Amanda asked, placing a slice of coconut cake onto a brown plate.

Sarah poured Amanda a cup of coffee and walked it over to the kitchen table. "I'm not sure," she confessed.

Amanda sat down across from Sarah, said a prayer of thanks for her food, and then looked at poor Mittens. Mittens was snoring away. "You gave the poor dear her medicine, didn't you?"

"Manford helped," Sarah told Amanda and took a sip of her coffee. "June Bug, I'm not sure how to reach the guy," she said in a miserable voice. "He's so...knotted up inside. There's a war taking place inside of his heart."

"And let me guess," Amanda said, taking a bite of her cake, "the little guy is his own worst enemy?"

Sarah nodded her head. "I'm afraid so."

Amanda munched on her cake and then washed the bite down with a sip of delicious coffee. "What's your plan, love?"

"Kill Manford with kindness, I suppose," Sarah replied. She grew silent and listened to the storm outside. "I'm glad you're here, June Bug. I don't like it when you're alone at your cabin."

"Me either," Amanda agreed in a serious voice. "I suppose I'm relatively safe at my cabin, but after all the monsters we've fought, I...well, every sound makes me jump. At times I imagine someone is at my bedroom window...scratching on the glass with dead fingers."

"Oh, June Bug."

"I know, I know," Amanda moaned. "I can't help it, Los Angeles. Every little sound makes my imagination drink ten cups of coffee at once." Amanda took another sip of coffee. "I'm okay during the daylight hours but when night falls and I'm all alone, sitting in the living room watching Jeopardy...oh my, every little sound makes me run for my gun. And when that happens," Amanda added, "I become furious with my hubby, because he should be home protecting me instead of off licking the boots of his daddy."

"He's taking care of family," Sarah reminded her. Sarah

reached across the table and patted Amanda's hand. "We have each other, June Bug."

Amanda allowed a weak smile to touch her face. "I know, love, but husbands are meant to be part of the team, too. Sadly, my bloke is far, far away. But," Amanda said, trying to cheer up, "at least my son came to visit me for a quick holiday and not one single thing went wrong."

"You have a lovely son, honey," Sarah smiled. "Your son has a good head on his shoulders and will do well in his life."

"My son has my smarts," Amanda told Sarah and then rolled her eyes. "My son has to have my smarts because if he had the brains of my dear hubby, he would be too dumb to know it's tea time when the kettle's steaming in his face!"

Sarah grinned. She got a kick out of Amanda fussing about her husband. "I'm sure your husband will be home soon."

"Next week...hopefully," Amanda told Sarah. "He's supposedly getting sick of being his dear old daddy's butler. Of course, I've heard that routine from his mouth before."

"Honey," Sarah asked, "how sick...I mean, really sick, is your father in law?"

Amanda threw her hands up in the air and rolled her

eyes. "Love, your guess is as good as mine. According to my hubby, the mean old goat has one foot in the grave."

"But according to your son?" Sarah asked as she worked on her coffee.

Amanda shook her head in disgust. "According to my son the mean old goat has years left in him. I have to agree with my son, love. But my dear old hubby...he may be brave when facing a bear, but he's sure spineless when it comes to facing down his daddy."

"Well, you still have me," Sarah said, trying to make her best friend feel better.

"And short stuff, your newest project," Amanda attempted to joke, nodding at the hallway leading to the closed bathroom door. She took a bite of her cake. "I suppose we all have our problems in life, don't we, love?"

Sarah watched a few crumbs fall from Amanda's mouth and smiled. "We sure do...like getting crumbs on a pretty new pink blouse and gray dress."

Amanda glanced down, spotted the crumbs that had fallen on her blouse, and brushed them away. "Crumbs are the least of my worries, love," she said and nodded toward the door leading out of the kitchen. "That little man has me worried."

"You're worried Manford is connected to Mrs. Appleson's murder?"

Amanda nodded her head. "I'm afraid so. I mean, let's face it, love, the chips sure aren't falling in the little guy's favor."

"No, they sure aren't," Sarah agreed, but then quickly assured Amanda that she didn't believe Manford had any involvement in the murder of Mrs. Appleson. "I don't think the murder is connected to me, either," she continued. "I'm sure in time we might find out that Mrs. Appleson had a few skeletons in her closet, maybe some that are still tied to some people she tried to escape from."

Amanda stared at Sarah with curious eyes. "Do you really think that's the answer, love?" she asked in an anxious voice. "Do you really think that cranky old bat had enemies?"

"One enemy in particular," Sarah nodded her head.

"Who?" Amanda begged, sitting on the edge of her seat.

"Macy Appleson."

"The daughter?" Amanda gasped.

Sarah nodded her head. "Conrad told me Macy Appleson was a failed actress who came up here from Los Angeles to find herself, whatever that means. I think there's more to it than that."

"Money?"

"Yep," Sarah said and finished off her coffee. "I think I'll get a refill." As Sarah stood up, Manford appeared in the kitchen door. "Oh...hello."

Amanda swung around in her seat and saw Manford wearing a dark gray sweater and pair of brown pants she had chosen to buy him. To her relief, the clothes she pulled from the boys clothing section in O'Mally's seemed to fit Manford, somewhat. He had cuffed the bottoms of the pants, which were a few inches too long, and the sweater was a tad too big, but nothing too disastrous. "You look very nice."

Manford looked down at himself and wiggled his toes inside the thick, warm, gray winter socks. "I like the socks the most," he said and then, in his own uneasy way, thanked Amanda for his gifts. "I...it's better to be warm than cold. Uh...thanks, you know."

"You're welcome...cutie," Amanda told Manford and tipped him a wink. Manford blushed. "Your boots are parked at the back door. I took the initiative and laced them for you."

Manford spotted a pair of sturdy, insulated brown boots beside the back door. "Go try on your boots," Sarah urged Manford. "I'll pour you a cup of coffee."

Manford bit down on his lip. "I...uh..."

"And try on your new coat, too," Amanda told Manford. She pointed to a green winter coat hanging on the coat rack that looked warm enough to keep a grizzly bear nice and toasty.

He hesitated again at the embarrassment of riches.

"Go ahead," Sarah smiled.

Manford shook his head. "I ain't used to people being nice to me. There's always strings attached."

"You bet there is," Sarah promised Manford. "You can wash dishes and bring in wood from the wood pile for me. Also," she added, "Mittens has to be walked when she goes outside to use the bathroom. At least for now, anyway. So that will be your chore."

Manford stared at the warm coat waiting for him. "Yeah, okay...I guess that's fair," he said and carefully retrieved his boots, sat down next to the kitchen door, and tried them on. "A size too big but they'll do," he told Amanda.

"I can exchange them for a smaller size."

"No, no..." Manford objected. "My mother said it's always good to let your toes have breathing room." Manford stood up, tested out the boots, and then retrieved his new coat and put it on over his new clothes. "Hey...warm...and there's room to move in here."

Sarah tossed Amanda a loving look. "Thank you," she whispered.

"Anytime, love," Amanda whispered back.

Manford pulled the hood over his head. "This is nice."

"Look in the pockets," Amanda smiled at Manford. Manford reached his hands into the pockets of his coat and pulled out a thick pair of winter gloves, a gray winter hat and a pair of black earmuffs. "Now when you walk Mittens or go outside to get wood from the wood pile, you'll be nice and warm."

Manford stared at the items in his hand. As he did, he felt an odd sensation grip his heart. The sensation terrified him. What in the world was he feeling? But suddenly he knew: Manford Sappers was feeling...gratitude. The two women he had attempted to rob honestly, sincerely cared about him. But why? He was a nobody. A nothing. A first-class street bum. Why would two lovely women care about him? His mind tried to argue the reason two strange women were caring about him was because he was a freak in their eyes. But somehow Manford knew there was more to it than what his mind was trying to press down on him. "Uh...thanks for everything."

"You're welcome...hot stuff," Amanda teased Manford.

Manford felt his cheeks turn red. "Okay...cut it out."

Sarah laughed, poured Manford a cup of coffee, and walked over to the table. "Want another slice of cake?"

"I already ate half of the cake," Manford told Sarah and patted his tummy. "I ate three of those turkey sandwiches with chips, too. I'm good for now."

Sarah smiled. "Come have some coffee."

Manford took off his coat, hung it up, and then looked around. "Uh...where are my...street clothes?"

"In the wash, as promised," Sarah assured Manford. "We can throw them away anytime you want."

"Not a chance," Manford said. He walked over to the table, climbed into a chair, and sat down. "I ain't staying in the snow forever, you know. Manford Sappers has...places to go...people to see. I'm just resting my feet for a bit, that's all."

Amanda tossed Sarah a worried look. Sarah shrugged her shoulders, refilled her coffee mug, and sat down. "Where are you planning to go next?" she asked Manford. "You're not exactly near a jumping metropolis."

"Yeah, you're way out in the Alaskan wilderness," Amanda added. "There's no taxi service or bus service in Snow Falls. The closest town you're going to find that has life in it is far, far away."

"Fairbanks," Sarah explained. "There's nothing between Snow Falls and Fairbanks except small communities like the one we live in." Sarah stared at Manford and began wondering how the little man had arrived in Snow Falls to begin with. Did he have a car? Did someone drop him off? Surely, he didn't walk...or did he? Maybe he hitchhiked? She had to know. But not yet. It wasn't time to push at Manford. First, she had to earn Manford's trust

—if that was possible—and prove to him that it was alright to trust in other people. Clothing and food and a hot shower were only the start. "I guess what we're saying is...Fairbanks isn't exactly a hop, skip and a jump from here."

Manford knew as much. He had stuck out his thumb all the way from Fairbanks to Snow Falls. Of course, he didn't know the first thing about Snow Falls but came to rest in the town after a kind man who was driving to some remote hunting lodge located in a faraway northern corner of the state dropped Manford off at an abandoned gas station near the county line. "Have to stop and see my sister for a few hours," the hunter told Manford. "Sure you don't want a ride into Snow Falls?" Manford shook his head. "Suit yourself. Someone should be along shortly. I'm sure you'll get a ride." Manford thanked the hunter for the ride and watched him drive away in his truck, leaving tire tracks on a snow-covered road. "Now what?" Manford asked, throwing his eyes right and left, and only seeing snow-caked woods. "I don't even know where I am." With no money in his pocket and a hard, icy wind blowing in his face, Manford started walking, cursing himself for not accepting the hunter's ride into town. Then he came up on an empty rental cabin a few miles down the road and decided to break inside. "I'll hide out here," he said, shivering from top to bottom, "at least it's safe." But soon hunger overcame Manford and he knew it was either find food or die, so he dared go into town and came upon O'Mally's department store. That's when he saw Sarah and Amanda get out of a jeep and start walking toward the front entrance. "Got to do it...now or never," he said, hiding behind a truck. Then he took out his hunting knife and allowed himself to become the lowest of lows.

"Manford?" Sarah asked. "Are you okay?"

"Huh?" Manford asked. He shook his head. "Sure, I'm good. I was just...you know, thinking."

"About what?" Sarah asked.

"About...how I can get myself some wheels," Manford lied. The truth was that he didn't know how to drive, but he didn't want Sarah or Amanda to discover that fact. He had to be tough—hard as rock and mean as a grizzly bear. Being soft was no good. "I need a...motorcycle. Yeah, that's the ticket."

"And do what? Join a biker gang?" Amanda asked.

"Maybe," Manford snapped, grabbed his coffee, and took a drink. He burned his tongue but didn't care. Sometimes being tough meant working through the pain. "I'll go outside and get some wood."

"Woodpile is in the backyard," Sarah told Manford and offered him a warm smile. "The wood holder is in the living room next to the fireplace."

"Yeah, I kinda figured that," Manford told Sarah. He took

another drink of coffee, burned his tongue for a second time, climbed down from his chair and went outside. "Gotta be tough...can't be soft...gotta be tough..." he told himself, though he felt shaky at the thought of running further. "Can't let Henry find me...can't let these two dames get to me...gotta be tough...gotta be tough."

Only, Manford was tired of being tough. Deep down inside of his heart, all he wanted to do was lay his head on Sarah's lap and cry.

———

Night arrived. Inside the darkness, a vicious storm growled over the little town of Snow Falls, threatening to knock down trees and cut power. But inside Sarah's cabin, a toasty fire was playing in a stone fireplace, casting warmth and light into a safe living room that smelled of pumpkin pie and popcorn. "Okay," Conrad said and rolled up the sleeves of his black sweater, "what movie are we going to watch, guys?" he asked.

Amanda, curled on the couch with a blanket and a bowl of popcorn, glanced over at the chair and saw Manford snoring away. "He's asleep," she whispered to Sarah.

Sarah turned away from the warm fire and looked at Manford. The poor dear was asleep, wrapped up in a warm green blanket, looking much younger than a twenty-something man. "Conrad...look."

Conrad turned from the bookcase against the wall and saw the sleeping Manford. "So much for a movie," he sighed and touched the bottom shelf of the bookcase with his boot. The bottom shelf of bookcase was home to a collection of classic black and white movies that Conrad loved to watch. He always watched his favorite black and white movies after dealing with a bad day.

Sarah walked over to Conrad and hugged his arm. "We can go into the kitchen and play Scrabble."

"No way," Amanda objected. "Conrad cheats."

"I do not cheat," Conrad growled. "You're just a poor loser...English crumpet girl. Little Miss Crumpet sat on her...uh...trumpet..."

"Oh, insult the little British girl," Amanda complained. "That doesn't even make sense. Do you even know what a crumpet is?"

"Hush, you two," Sarah demanded. "You'll wake Manford." Sarah ushered Conrad into the kitchen and motioned for Amanda to follow. Amanda sighed, put down her bowl of popcorn, removed the blanket from around her lap, and made her way into the kitchen. "Now listen," Sarah said, "the pumpkin pie I'm baking is almost ready. We'll have pie and play Scrabble, okay?"

Amanda glared at Conrad and then raised a warning finger at him. "No funny words, leather jacket boy."

Conrad plopped down at the kitchen table. "No slang words from London, either, Miss Crumpet," he warned.

Sarah grinned. "You two are impossible."

Amanda grinned. "Yes, we are."

Conrad began to speak but stopped when the phone rang. "That's probably Andrew," he said. "I'll answer it." Conrad stood up, walked to the phone hanging beside the refrigerator, and answered the call. "Hello?"

"Is this Detective Conrad Spencer?" a voice asked in a strange tone of voice.

"Uh...yes, it is. Who is this?" Conrad asked.

The man drew in a deep breath and exhaled cheap cigar smoke among the scent of wet hay and stale popcorn. "Detective Spencer, my name is Henry Billinger. I'm the owner of Nine Clowns Circus," Henry explained. He began pacing back and forth in a miserable, small trailer covered with old circus posters and furnished with only a worn-down brown couch and a chipped yellow table on green linoleum that was badly peeling at the corners of the room.

Conrad threw his eyes at Sarah. Sarah read his eyes and rushed over to the phone. "What can I do for you, Mr. Billinger?" he asked and eased the phone away from his ear enough for Sarah to hear.

Henry grabbed a cheap cigar from the filthy ashtray on

the table and hiked his pants up over his substantial belly. "Detective Spencer, I'm searching for a missing employee. I received word that this employee might be in Alaska. I've been calling every town searching for him. Your town was next on my list," he explained. "I was told to call this number since you were not available at the station." Henry grabbed a pack of matches from his shirt pocket and ripped one off, using it to relight the cigar. At the age of fifty, Henry was fully aware that out of his ringmaster suit and costume, he was nothing more than a fat man with thinning gray hair and a face that would scare a lion away, whip or no whip. But Henry didn't care about his appearance. All he cared about was money, and that came from power—the power he held over his circus. Getting Manford Sappers back into the fold before it was too late was even more important than power right now. "I've been coming up empty-handed, I'm afraid. Maybe you can help me?"

Conrad glanced at Sarah. Sarah bit down on her lip. "Who are you looking for, Mr. Billinger?"

Henry took a puff from his cheap cigar. He felt tired. Calling every town in the state of Alaska was tiring work. "I'm searching for a man named Manford Sappers, Detective. This man has stolen a great deal of money from me and I'm anxious to get my money back without involving the law. You see, I'm a peaceful man, Detective, and believe in giving all of my employees a second chance," Henry said in a sickening, wheedling voice that made Conrad feel like he wanted to take a bleach bath.

Sarah locked her eyes on the kitchen door and then waved her hand at Amanda. "Go keep an eye on Manford," she told Amanda. Amanda hurried out of the kitchen.

"Your Chief of Police sent me in your direction, Detective," Henry continued.

Conrad put on a more official tone of voice. "What does this man look like, Mr. Billinger?" he asked as the storm winds howled and cried outside. Mittens raised her head and focused on Conrad's intent face.

"Well, Detective," Henry said, puffing on his cheap cigar, "Manford Sappers isn't your ordinary man. Manford is a circus person," Henry said in a voice that sounded like a slithery snake.

"What does that mean?" Conrad insisted. "Mr. Billinger, I've had a busy day and I don't have time to play Guess Who. Just give me the description of this Manford Sappers person and I'll keep an eye out."

Henry frowned. He didn't like being spoken to like this, especially not by some two-bit backwoods sheriff type. "Alright, I'll speak plain. Manford Sappers is a little person," he snapped. "A little person thief that stole my money. I want it back."

"A little person?" Conrad asked. "Don't get many of that description in Snow Falls. I'll keep an eye out, Mr. Billinger."

"You do that," Henry snapped again and slammed the phone down onto the scarred table on its last legs.

Conrad hung up the phone. "You played that very well. Thank you," Sarah said and hugged Conrad.

Conrad put his arm around Sarah. "Looks like we have a few more answers to our mystery," he said and studied the kitchen door. "I guess we better go speak with our guest."

Sarah let go of Conrad, looked toward the back door, and listened to the storm. "I suppose tonight would be a good night. I don't think Manford would try to run in this storm. If we wait until morning he might try to run."

"After you, then."

Sarah sighed. Confronting Manford wasn't going to be easy. "Okay," she said and walked back to the living room. She found Amanda standing near the fireplace. Manford was still sound asleep. "Oh, I hate to wake him. He must be exhausted."

"Then let me," Conrad said. He walked to the sitting chair and bumped it with his right thigh. "Manford...Manford...you need to wake up, buddy."

Manford's eyes flew open. Panic grabbed his face. He

threw his head to the left and then to the right, and then jumped up from the chair, unaware of the blanket wrapped around him. He became tangled up in the folds of the blanket and crashed down to the floor. "Let me go...let me go...don't hurt me...let me go!" he cried.

Sarah felt her heart break. She ran to Manford and grabbed his shoulders. "Manford...it's me, Sarah...no one is going to hurt you. It's okay."

"Let me go...don't hurt me!" Manford yelled and began fighting against Sarah. "Let me go!"

"Manford...calm down, honey. It's Sarah...look at me...look at me!" Sarah grabbed Manford's face and forced him to look at her. "It's me...you're okay."

Manford stared at Sarah with fear-stricken eyes. Slowly his mind began to crawl into the land of consciousness. "Sarah...?"

Sarah nodded her head. "You...I guess you were having a bad dream." Sarah shot an upset look at Conrad. Conrad winced. How was he supposed to know Manford would wake up in a panicked state of mind?

Manford felt his heart racing. "I...uh..." he said, struggling to wake up. "Yeah...guess so," he finished and looked down at the blanket he was wrapped in. "Help me out of this thing?"

Sarah nodded her head and began helping Manford out

of the tangled blanket. "Better?" she asked and placed the blanket down onto the sitting chair.

"I guess," Manford said. She gave him a hand so he could stand up and sit back down on the armchair. He looked around and spotted Amanda standing beside the fireplace and Conrad standing close to the bookcase. "Uh...what's with everyone?" he asked.

Sarah braced herself. "Manford, a man by the name of Mr. Billinger just called—"

"Henry Billinger?" Manford gasped in fear and panic. He threw his eyes toward the front door and started to run.

"Oh no," Sarah said and grabbed Manford's shoulder. "I'm not letting you go out into that storm to die."

Manford pulled away from Sarah. "If I stay here, I'll die for sure!" he yelled. "Henry will kill me!"

"Henry Billinger doesn't know you're in Snow Falls," Sarah tried to calm down Manford. "He's calling every town in Alaska, asking around for you. We told him you weren't here."

"My wife is telling you the truth," Conrad told Manford. He drew in a deep breath and folded his arms. Against his better judgment, he was allowing Manford Sappers to work on his heart. Why? Maybe it was because he saw goodness in Manford—a deep, hidden goodness that only a good cop could see. "Buddy, no one is going to hurt you."

"Henry Billinger will kill me," Manford insisted in a desperate voice. "I...he..." Manford threw his eyes up at Sarah. "I..."

"You what?" Sarah asked. "Talk to me. Why are you so afraid of him? Tell us, and maybe we can help you."

Manford saw a tear fall from Sarah's eyes. The woman was genuinely worried for him. No one besides his own mother had ever really worried for him before. "I..." Manford said, feeling Sarah's tear melt his tough heart. "I..." Manford tried to speak but instead, to his own shock, he collapsed down into himself on the chair and sobbed. "I'm scared..." he cried and began shaking all over.

Sarah threw her arms around Manford as tears began flooding from her eyes. "I know...I know," she said in a loving voice. She pulled Manford close and held him. "No one is going to hurt you. I promise."

"Henry will kill me," Manford cried. "Henry vowed to hunt me down and kill me. That's why I ran...I had to get away from him...I came here all the way from New York." Manford kept his head tucked into Sarah's tummy. "I used all the money I had and jumped a flight to Anchorage. It's been rough travel ever since."

Sarah smoothed Manford's rumpled hair out of his eyes.

"I know it has. But now you have...you have friends here who want to help you."

Manford raised his eyes. "I don't have anyone," he said as tears dripped from his scared eyes.

"You do now," Sarah promised and kissed Manford's forehead.

"You bet you do," Amanda said, wiping away her own tears. She ran to Manford and hugged him from the other side. "I'll kill the first person who ever tries to lay a hand on you."

Conrad walked up to Manford and looked right into his eyes. "Look at me," he said. Manford dared to raise his eyes. "If my wife trusts you, then I trust you. My life before yours," Conrad promised Manford. "You have family now. Is that clear?"

Manford stared into Conrad's eyes and saw that the cop—a cop who usually would have dismissed him as a deadbeat loser—meant his words. "I..." he tried to speak but couldn't find the words. Instead, he threw his face back into Sarah's shoulder and cried.

After a moment, Sarah looked up at her husband and her best friend. "Leave us alone for a moment...please," Sarah begged.

Amanda wiped at her tears. "Come on, you, we'll go play Scrabble. I'll even let you cheat."

"I'll make the coffee," Conrad told Amanda and walked her away.

Sarah took Manford's hand and sat him down on the couch. "Okay, we need to talk," she said and wiped her tears away. "This Henry Billinger person claimed you stole money from him. Is that true?"

Manford glanced down at his lap. "I didn't steal anything. That money belonged to my mother," he whispered. "The money was her back wages that Henry refused to give me when...she died."

"What did you do with the money?" Sarah asked. She slowly sat down next to Manford, keeping an arm around his shoulders.

"I couldn't take it all...it was too much, and I was scared, I had to get out of town quick. So I buried most of the money near my mother's grave," Manford explained as fresh tears began falling from his eyes. He felt weak but couldn't stop his tears from escaping. "Mom deserved the money. The money was hers...not Henry's."

Sarah brushed his hair away from his eyes. "I think I understand."

"No, you don't," Manford insisted, pulling himself out of her grasp and scooting away, glaring. "You don't understand anything. You don't understand how cruel my old man was to me and my mother for so many years...how he dragged us around from one crummy town

77

to another while Henry Billinger tormented us...you don't understand how many hungry nights I spent...how many nights I held my mother while she cried herself to sleep and I tried to shield her body with my own in case my old man came home drunk again. You don't know how many times I stole for food...stupid, lousy food..." Manford threw his hands over his face and knuckled the tears out of his eyes again.

Sarah wanted to gently wrap her arms around him, to hold Manford the way a loving mother would hold her scared child. She wanted to give him back some of what he had lost—but all she could offer him was friendship, and shelter, and safety. She hoped it was enough. It would have to be enough.

Far away in New York, Henry Billinger stared at the bitter end of his cheap cigar, wondering how many little Alaskan dumps he would have to call before he would find that rotten thief, when the telephone in his trailer rang. "Hello?" he barked.

"Mr. Billinger, this is Officer Jenkins with the White Owl Police Department in Alaska. You called me earlier looking for a Mr. Sappers?"

"Yes...yes, I did," Henry said, feeling hope rush through his veins. "You've found my man?"

"No, not exactly," Officer Jenkins replied. "But one of my guys said he thought he saw someone fitting the description of the man you're looking for. He saw a little person get picked up by a man who lives in town."

"Do tell," Henry grinned and licked his lips, greedy for details.

"Well, it may not be much, but this fella was leaving town to go up north on a hunting trip. He always stops in a town called Snow Falls to see his sister first. I'm the closest town to Snow Falls out this way and there isn't a town after Snow Falls. If I were you, I would call Andrew over in Snow Falls, he's the Chief of Police, and see if your man has turned up there."

"Oh, I will, I will," Henry promised. "You've been of great help, officer. Great help indeed."

CHAPTER FOUR

Manford woke up in a warm, soft bed, a strange sensation that stirred uneasiness in his limbs, at first. He slowly opened his eyes and spotted a window covered with a dark green drape. Outside the window he heard an icy wind exploring a gentle world of white snow. Then he remembered where he was—safe and warm in Sarah's cabin—and he drifted back to sleep. But the safe feeling dissipated when he fell into a dark nightmare. Inside the nightmare, he saw himself standing inside of a filthy circus tent, on a familiar red wooden box positioned in the middle of the main circus ring. The reek of decaying hay was everywhere, mixed in with the familiar fug of elephant dung, stale peanut hulls and wadded-up greasy popcorn boxes. A spotlight shone down, and thousands upon thousands of eyes stared at him from the dark beyond, pinning him in place, a freak on display with nowhere to run. He tried to move and found his feet were chained, glued in place. "No...let me go!" he cried and tried to pull away, and the faces in the darkness only laughed to see him struggle. "Let me go...please!"

"Manford...oh, Manford..." a voice crawled out of the darkness surrounding the circus ring, "why did you betray me, Manford? Why did you run?" A dim shadow with a tall hat and a shabby suit loomed toward him.

"Leave me alone!" Manford cried and began trying to free his feet from the chains. That's when he noticed he wore the clothes Amanda had bought him, but his feet were still stuck in the run-down shoes he had been wearing when the hunter dropped him off in Snow Falls. "Leave me alone..."

"Oh, Manford...it's time to pay your bill," the creepy voice hissed. "Look."

Manford threw his eyes to the side and saw a fierce, hungry lion slowly stalk toward him out of the darkness. The lion let out a loud roar and swiped a vicious paw at Manford. "No...please...don't let him eat me...please let me go...please..." Manford begged as the lion stalked closer and closer to him, its eyes gleaming. As the lion drew closer, its face began to change. To Manford's horror, he saw the face of Henry Billinger appear. "No!"

"Time to pay your bill, Manford!" Henry roared at Manford with vicious, hungry teeth.

"No...let me go...don't hurt me...let me go...let me go!" Manford cried.

Sarah rushed into the guest room at the noise, spotted Manford struggling with the warm green quilt covering his body, and dashed over to the bed. "Manford...you're having a nightmare...Manford, wake up," she begged and began shaking Manford's shoulders. "Manford...honey...it's only a nightmare...wake up...wake up."

Inside the circus ring, Manford heard Sarah's sweet voice float out of the darkness. The lion jerked its head up, sniffed the air, and let out an ominous feline hiss. "You'll be back," he warned Manford. "You'll never escape this ring!"

Manford watched as the lion backed away into the darkness. As the lion backed away, a bright, warm light appeared over his head. He looked up and saw two loving hands reaching down from the light to break the chains wrapped around his feet and snatch him away...up...up...and up. Manford closed his eyes as he was being snatched up.

When he finally opened his eyes, he saw Sarah's beautiful face leaning down over him. "Sarah?" he whispered, still hoarse.

"It's me...you were having a nightmare," Sarah explained in a soft voice as she quickly brushed Manford's sweaty hair away from his eyes and offered him a sweet, strong smile. "I was in the kitchen with Conrad making breakfast and I heard you. Hungry?"

Manford lay very still and stared up at Sarah. "Your voice came out of the darkness. You ran off the lion," he whispered.

"Oh?" Sarah asked, uncertain what Manford meant, but she decided to pretend she understood. "Well then, that's a good thing."

"More than you know," Manford promised Sarah in a grateful voice. He let out a deep sigh and looked toward the window. "What time is it?"

"Almost nine o'clock," Sarah explained. "The storm has passed...about four this morning. I heard the first snow plow out about ten minutes ago." Sarah patted Manford's hand. "I thought we could drive to O'Mally's today and get you some more clothes?"

"What for?" Manford asked.

Sarah smiled and motioned around the guest room with her eyes. "If you're going to live here, you're going to need more than one change of clothes."

"Live...here?" Manford asked in a confused voice. He leaned up in the bed and stared at Sarah with shock.

"That's right," Conrad said. Manford shot his eyes to the right and saw Conrad leaning against the bedroom door, wearing his usual leather jacket and sipping on a cup of coffee. The guy looked stealthy but solid, comforting. "Sarah and I have been talking. We've decided that we want you to live with us, Manford. We want you to make Snow Falls your home," he explained in a sincere voice that shocked Manford to the core. The tough cop had a tender heart.

Sarah nodded her head. "Conrad and I want you to become part of our family," she told Manford, gently leaned forward, kissed his forehead, and stood up. "The choice is yours, of course, but we pray you choose to accept us as your family," she finished.

Manford couldn't believe his ears. He stared up at Sarah in shock. Sarah smiled and motioned at the pink bathrobe she was wearing. "Amanda is hogging the bathroom. I guess I need to go run her out and get dressed for the day. Breakfast is in the kitchen, okay?"

"Uh...okay."

Sarah walked out of the guest room, leaving Conrad alone with Manford. Conrad studied Manford with concerned eyes. He wanted the guy to become part of their family but feared the world had created a distrust in him that would never abate. "Manford," he said in a careful voice, easing into the bedroom and sitting down in a chair in front of an antique writing desk, "I meant what I said. I want you to become part of our little family of friends up here in Snow Falls. I understand we're still strangers to each other, but in time that can change." Conrad set down his coffee. "I'm not going to sit here and pretend I'm perfect...neither is Sarah. I'm sure at times we'll fuss with each other and have some arguments. But that's what families do, right?"

"I...my mom and me...we argued at times," Manford nodded his head.

"My old man...we sure had some fights," Conrad nodded. "I never stopped loving my old man, though. He was tough...and hard to know, but he cared." Conrad glanced around the guest room. The guest room was just right for Manford. "You can change this room into your own...you know, make it...cool."

Manford began to speak but felt a sharp piece of glass cut into his thoughts and slice all his good feelings to ribbons. "I...I'm a grown man. I can take care of myself and I don't need no charity, okay?" he said in a voice that didn't hold an inch of conviction. After breaking down in front of Sarah and holding onto the woman like she was his actual mother, all of his defenses broke; and he felt glad for that.

"Love isn't charity," Conrad answered Manford simply.

Manford stared at Conrad in shock as the three simple words the man spoke thundered into his heart: Love Isn't Charity. Those three words shook his mind, grabbed the cruel piece of glass digging into his thoughts, and yanked it away. "I guess not," he said and actually felt a smile touch his face. "I guess I should go walk Mittens, right?"

"I already did," Conrad smiled back and tipped Manford a wink. "In this house you'll learn, the same way I did, that the women go before the men do."

Manford grinned. He sure liked Conrad. Maybe not at first—especially when Conrad handcuffed him—but now it was clear that Conrad was a real cool, decent guy with a good heart to him; honest, too. "I guess so."

Conrad felt relief sweep through his heart. He stood up, walked over to the bed, and sat down on the edge. "Manford," he said in a sincere voice, "I never had children and I'm not really old enough to be your old man. All I can offer you is my friendship, my loyalty and my...well...you know, my devotion to family. I'm not a drinker, a yeller or a hitter...well, I do hit the bad guys. Sometimes I'll take a walk and smoke a cigar and when I get upset, I'll watch some of my old movies." Conrad steadied himself. "I'm a man who loves his wife, is devoted to his work, and enjoys his life here in Snow Falls, even though...at times, I miss Brooklyn...but don't tell Sarah that."

"Why are you telling me this stuff?" Manford asked.

Conrad patted Manford's arm. "I believe in being honest from the start," he explained. "I want you to know what you're getting from the get-go...no surprises later on, you know?"

"I guess that's kinda cool of you to do," Manford confessed.

Conrad glanced down at his leather jacket. "Being cool comes from what's inside of you, not the outside," he explained and tossed Manford a smile. "Hey, I better get to the station and see what our Chief of Police is doing. You have a good day, okay?"

"I will. And..." Manford stopped. His eyes suddenly grew wide with fear. "What about Henry?" he begged.

Conrad patted Manford's arm again. "Sarah and Amanda have dealt with the worst mankind has to offer," he said. "She and Amanda took down the Back Alley Killer together. Those two are tough as rocks and they've been thrown over more cliffs than I can count, without budging an inch. If...and this is a big if...if this Henry Billinger character shows up in town, they'll take him on, and so will I. We're not going to let him drag you off somewhere you don't want to go. But in the meantime... what we're not going to do is let you live your life in fear, okay?"

"I...but Henry—"

"Buddy, you're safe now," Conrad promised. "And if danger does peek its dark head up at you, well, you have people who will stand beside you and fight." Conrad stood up. "Now do me a favor."

"A favor?"

"Yeah," Conrad scratched the back of his head. "Sarah kinda has this big day planned for you. She wants to take you to O'Mally's, show you her coffee shop, take you to the diner, and finish off the day with a walk in the snow. So...humor her, okay?"

"I heard that," Sarah shouted from her bedroom.

Conrad winced. "Woman has ears like an owl."

"I heard that, too!"

Conrad winced again. "I better get to the station. I still have a murder case to solve," he told Manford in a quick voice and dashed away to the kitchen.

Manford felt a grin touch his worried face. It was clear to him that Sarah and Conrad were soulmates. He sure wished he had a soulmate—a woman to love and devote his heart to. "Maybe...things can change?" he whispered and looked toward the bedroom window. "Maybe...this can be a new beginning for me? Sure, Alaska isn't New York...but I'm not tied to New York. Maybe what I need is a fresh new start...in the snow?"

"Maybe," Sarah said, peeking her head into the guest room, "the snow is exactly what you need?"

"Wow...you do have ears like an owl," Manford said, startled and turning.

Sarah smiled. "What do you think?" she asked and smoothed out the dark blue dress she had put on. "I still need to do my hair...so just look at the dress."

Manford thought Sarah was the most beautiful woman he had ever seen—besides his own mother. As a matter of fact, he thought, Sarah sure looked a lot like his mother...just way taller. "I think...you look...beautiful." Manford drew in a deep, nervous breath and blurted out: "Just like my mom."

"Then I'm very honored," Sarah blushed. "Now, why don't you get dressed and come eat breakfast. I cooked you an omelet, some pancakes, hot oatmeal, turkey sausage, hash browns and toast."

"I helped," Amanda said from the bathroom. "All Conrad did was peel the potatoes."

"All you did was crack the eggs," Conrad hollered from the kitchen.

"Go to work already!" Amanda said, coming out to the hallway and grinning at Sarah and Manford. "And be careful, you silly Yankee man," she added in a mutter.

"Yes, dear," Conrad said and then added: "I'll see you all at the diner for dinner at six."

"Love you!" Sarah called out.

"Love you more!" Conrad called back and slipped out of the back door but then stuck his head back in and yelled: "Manford?"

"Uh...yeah?"

"Can you come and help me dig out my truck?" Conrad asked.

Sarah rolled her eyes. "Conrad, Manford needs to eat breakfast."

"No, no...I'll...I love to help. Shoveling snow will work up my appetite."

Sarah sighed. "Okay. If you say so. I'll keep it warm for you."

Manford actually smiled. "I kinda need to...get dressed."

"Oh...oh, yeah." Sarah rushed away and closed the door.

Manford jumped out of bed, got dressed, ran his fingers through his messy hair, hurried to the back door, slapped on his coat, gloves and earmuffs, and stepped outside into snowdrifts almost up to his waist. "Conrad?" he said, closing the back door.

"Over here!" Conrad yelled, stepping out of a wooden work shed carrying two snow shovels. He trudged through the snow and made his way to Manford. "Here you go."

"Thanks," Manford said, taking a green snow shovel from

Conrad. He walked his eyes around the white winter landscape and let out a white trail of breath. The gentle winds were very icy, and it felt cold enough to freeze the Sahara deep into one giant iceberg, but he didn't care. All Manford saw before his eyes was beauty; Alaskan beauty that was untouched by man. "I never saw so much snow before."

Conrad leaned down on a red snow shovel. "Let me tell you," he said, breathing out white puffs of smoke, "the snow is great...but all this beauty sure can exact a toll on the old muscles." He stretched his shoulders a little beneath his thick jacket.

"Is it worth it? For the beauty of it, I mean?" Manford asked, feeling the icy winds grabbing at his cold face.

Conrad considered Manford's question. "You know, it is," he confessed and nodded his head. "Okay, let's dig out my truck."

Manford watched Conrad begin digging a path to the truck and then start on the back left side of his truck. He was grateful to realize that Conrad was not going to patronize him or think less of his physical abilities; he genuinely expected Manford, as another man, to carry his own load. He smiled, walked to the back of the truck, and began digging out the back right tire. Thirty minutes later, he handed Conrad the green snow shovel back, wiped sweat from his face, and nodded his head. "That should do it," he said in a proud voice.

Conrad studied his truck. The truck's wheels were clear, enough to reach the clear path that had been plowed partway from the road to the cabin. "You do good work," he said, and quickly yanked out his wallet.

"Hey...that's not necessary," Manford protested in a surprised voice.

Conrad handed Manford a twenty-dollar bill. "You earned every penny," he explained. "That's hard work, and you made my burden lighter this morning. No sense not paying you fairly for your labor."

Manford stared at the twenty-dollar bill. Instead of feeling like Conrad had tossed charity into his face, he felt...proud. "All this?"

"Why, sure."

Manford beamed. "Hey, this might be a good day after all."

Henry Billinger took a cab to John F. Kennedy airport and booked a ticket to Alaska, the words of the White Owl police officer echoing in his head. As he stood at the ticket counter buying his ticket, he contemplated what he would do when he found Manford and smiled in a way that discomforted the woman working the computer behind the desk. He shifted into a semblance of politeness and looked away. Closer and closer, he approached.

Thousands of miles away, Manford sat at Sarah's warm kitchen table gobbling down a delicious breakfast, listening to Amanda complain about her green dress with white polka dots; she was convinced the dress wasn't really her style, though Manford knew not to say a word as he listened to her chat away. "Oh, this dress was so lovely on the rack in London...like a springtime fantasy... but now look at me...I'm a frog with chicken pox."

Sarah burst out laughing. "You look fine," she said, nearly spilling her cup of coffee.

"What you mean is I look sillier than a garden toad with a rare disease," Amanda complained, took a sip of coffee, and then grabbed a banana muffin off a plate.

"That muffin was for Manford, honey."

"You snooze, you lose the muffin," Amanda told Manford and took a bite of the muffin. Manford grinned, already half-full and not begrudging her the muffin at all. Amanda was turning out to be a very interesting kind of woman.

"You're impossible, June Bug," Sarah laughed.

"An impossible woman? Or an impossible frog with an incurable case of deadly pox?"

Manford grinned, took a sip of coffee, and dug into a

stack of pancakes. It sure was nice having food in the morning instead of scrounging on the streets. "I'll go dig your jeep out after I'm finished eating," he told Sarah.

"Ah, a real gentleman," Amanda sighed. "You can't get that husband of yours to dig out your jeep without fussing up a storm."

"Oh, Conrad isn't that bad," Sarah responded and then quickly ducked her head down. "Sometimes. He's just...busy."

"Your darling hubby hates to shovel snow, love."

"Well...shoveling snow does get old," Sarah said, trying to defend Conrad. "And he usually does dig out his truck and my jeep every time it snows."

"I guess that's fair enough...for now," Amanda told Sarah and winked at Manford. "I like giving Conrad a difficult time. Deep down I do care for the bloke. But don't you ever tell him that."

"I won't," Manford said and, to his shock, tossed a wink back at Amanda. Now what in the world made him do that? Was he actually warming up to the woman, settling into this cozy little life? No way. Surely, he was the same Manford Sappers as he'd always been. He was just a tough guy...who needed family.

Sarah checked her watch. "Say, the morning is getting late on us."

"I'll hurry," Manford promised.

"You'll do no such thing," Sarah told Manford. "Take your time and eat. In the meantime, Amanda and I will go outside and shovel out my jeep and her truck."

"But I can—" Manford began to object.

"Manford," Sarah interrupted and quickly finished off her coffee, "I know you can shovel out my jeep, and I appreciate it. I'm not refusing your offer because I don't think you can. The truth is, I don't want you to feel you have to earn your place here. I want you to take your time and eat your breakfast...and then...walk around, get a feel for the place, make it your home. Please." Sarah stood up, patted Manford's hand, and nodded at Amanda. "Ready, June Bug?"

Amanda sighed. "Can I bring my muffin?"

Sarah giggled. "I suppose."

Amanda looked at Manford and placed her left hand over her forehead. "Alas, sweet prince, this princess shall now be taken prisoner by the hands of a cruel winter. Farewell...farewell."

Manford grinned. "Don't forget the snow behind the front tires."

Amanda's face froze, and then frowned. "Gee, what a way to treat royalty...thanks a lot."

Sarah put on her coat and then handed Amanda her coat. "Manford, hon, take your time," she begged. "It'll take us about half an hour to shovel the snow away."

"Okay," Manford said. He watched Sarah and Amanda leave the kitchen and trudge out into the snow, leaving him alone. Silence immediately dropped down from the ceiling like a hard hand. "Well," he told Mittens, "what do you think?" Mittens wagged her tail. Manford glanced around the warm kitchen and then looked down at his breakfast plate. "It isn't charity," he whispered. "Love is what matters...and these people are offering me love."

Manford stood up, stretched his back, and then decided to walk around the cabin. He explored the pantry, the kitchen, the living room, the bathroom, his room, and even peeked his head into Sarah's writing room. The cabin, without Sarah and Conrad present, felt empty and lonely—yet, everywhere Manford looked he saw the smiling faces of Sarah, Conrad and even Amanda. The coziness of their presence was what made the place so home-like and inviting and safe. "People matter," he whispered, walked back into the kitchen and to the back door. "People...really matter."

Manford spotted Sarah tossing a shovel of snow at Amanda.

"Hey...not funny!" Amanda yelled. She slapped snow off her face, dipped her own shovel into the snow, and prepared to cover Sarah from head to toe. Sarah giggled and quickly ran to the other side of her jeep. "You're not going to escape, love!"

"Come and get me, June Bug," Sarah giggled, unaware that Manford was watching from the kitchen.

Amanda eased to the back of the jeep and peeked around. Sarah giggled and moved to the front of the jeep. "I'm going to color you white with snow," Amanda called out in a corny sing-song that made Manford smile.

"Run, Sarah," Manford whispered. "Run—" Manford stopped when he heard the telephone ring. He slowly turned and looked at the telephone hanging beside the refrigerator. His heart began to race, and his palms began to sweat. "Stop," Manford scolded himself. "If that's...if this...well, if this is going to be my home, I have to stop being so afraid." Manford drew in a deep breath, walked over to the phone, and answered it. "Hello, Mrs. Spencer's home," he said, looking around for paper in case he had to write down a message.

"Why, hello Manford," Henry hissed, nearly peeing his pants with glee. His hideous grin stretched his entire face grotesquely, making a man walking past at just that moment shudder and recoil. Henry stepped into his assigned gate, walked over to a large glass window, and peered out at a jet. "Fancy finding you at this number."

Manford froze. Fear and panic squeezed his heart. "No. You..."

Henry watched a cold, hard rain falling onto the jet outside. The rain was threatening to turn icy, but the ticket agent had assured him that his flight would be well in the air before any weather cancellations began to take place. "You thought you could escape me, didn't you, you little rat? But I found you, didn't I? Oh yes, I did. And now I'm coming for you."

Manford nearly dropped the phone. "How..." he began to speak in a shaky voice and then stopped. He squeezed his eyes closed, saw Henry's creepy face on the deadly lion of his nightmares, and cringed all over. "You're...never going to get my mother's money back...no matter what...so leave me alone," he begged in a weak voice.

"I'm going to feed you to my lions, you little rat," Henry hissed, keeping his voice low. Even though he was dressed in a nice gray suit and had his hair slicked back, he still attracted some attention from the fellow passengers in the gate area, and he didn't want anyone hearing his conversation. "I'm going to make you pay, Manford. No one escapes Henry Billinger, do you hear me? Your old man didn't escape me...your precious mother didn't escape me...and you will not escape me. Only in death, you miserable rat, will you escape me, and trust me, my lions are waiting to help you make that particular escape."

Manford began to tremble all over. "You'll never find me. You—"

"I'm on my way to Snow Falls right now, you miserable thief. And when I arrive, I'm going to find you...one way or the other," Henry threatened. "You stole a great deal of money from me. The police are on my side," he lied. "I've already spoken to the Chief of Police and he has agreed to arrest you."

"You're lying," Manford said, stumbling over his own words. "Conrad...I mean, Detective Spencer didn't leave too long ago, and he said—"

Henry gritted his teeth. So Manford was chumming up with the cops, was he? Well, he had a solution for that. "The Chief of Police doesn't tell your precious Detective Spencer everything. Are you really that naïve? Do you think I'd find you and then let some idiot backwoods detective keep you from me? No. They won't shelter a criminal anyway. What lies have you been telling them?" He grinned, waiting in the stunned silence, hearing Manford's abject terror. It soothed Henry's ugly heart. "I'm going to have the Chief of Police arrest you and extradite you to New York. And guess who will escort you there? I'm going to take you back to New York personally and feed you to my lions."

"I'll run...I've been running, and I can do it again."

Henry gritted his teeth even harder. "If you dare run, I'll track down your sister and kill her. I'm through playing nice, do you hear me?"

"You don't know where my sister is," Manford told Henry in a terrified voice. "I don't even know. Mother hid her from you on purpose, she knew what kind of a man you are...she even hid my sister from me...from the world."

"Oh, I can find her...I will find her," Henry threatened Manford.

Manford wasn't sure if Henry was telling the truth or not. What Manford was sure of was that Henry Billinger was a psychotic madman obsessed with power and revenge—a creature who would never rest until he destroyed every innocent person he hungered to kill. "You'll never find my sister," he told Henry desperately. "I don't even know where my sister is, what her name is...nothing."

"Oh, I can find out, you little rat," Henry snapped. "Your mother was always sloppy. She left me a clear trail to follow...just like you did," he lied, knowing Manford had no idea he'd only found him by luck.

The idea of Henry Billinger tracking down Manford's sister had never occurred to him before: it sent a terrifying shudder all through him. Manford's mother had given up the girl for adoption at birth, terrified of bringing another child into the squalid, hopeless life of Billinger's circus; his mother had assured Manford that the people who had taken his sister would always protect her. But now he had no doubt that Henry Billinger would do whatever it took to find her, if he thought it would help him get Manford back, and the money back. "If you touch my sister...I'll..." he tried to speak in a scared voice. The truth...the tragic truth...was that Manford Sappers was terrified of Henry Billinger; terrified of the lions; terrified of the drudgery and misery of his circus life. He could not imagine going back. Yet it might be the only way to save his sister. "If you touch her, I'll—" he tried again, his voice failing.

"You'll what?" Henry hissed. "What will you do, you little rat? I fed your old man to my lions and I'm going to do the same to you. Oh yes," Henry grinned, "your old man tried to run away from me, too, and I found him. No one, you pathetic punk, runs from Henry Billinger and escapes, do you hear me?"

Manford heard the back door open. He jerked his head up, saw Sarah appear, drenched with snow, and froze. Sarah locked her eyes on Manford's face, stopped smiling, ran to the phone, and snatched it away. "Mr. Billinger, this is Detective Sarah Spencer," she said in a tough voice. "How dare you—"

"Ah, detective," Henry said, turning on his manipulative charm for the pretty voice. "I'm glad we're—"

"If you step one foot in Snow Falls, I'm going to arrest you, is that clear?" Sarah warned Henry, throwing the man into a fit of rage. "You are never, and I mean never, to come near Manford Sappers again. Do I make myself clear?"

"That little thief stole a great deal of money from me," Henry raged, causing other people sitting in the terminal to look at him. "I'll get him extradited! He owes me that money!"

"You must prove that in a court of law, Mr. Billinger, and if you do, the law will handle it. In the meantime, I will not tolerate threats against Manford. Criminal threats are a misdemeanor felony in Alaska: don't make me put out a warrant with your name on it. If you step a foot in this state, the state police will run your name and you won't even make it out of the airport. Am I making myself perfectly clear?"

Henry balled his left hand into a tight fist and gritted his teeth so hard that he thought they were going to turn to dust. "I will have justice...one way or the other. Am I making myself perfectly clear, woman?"

"Step one foot in Snow Falls and you'll get all the justice you want," Sarah warned Henry. "My husband and I are both detectives that know many people who sit in powerful positions. And not just in Alaska. Did you know my husband used to work in New York City for many years? We'll have every ounce of the law thrown at you, Mr. Billinger, until you can't move one step in any direction. We'll have the IRS audit your little circus, the Feds investigate your private life, and the local authorities following you everywhere you go. We'll have your circus shut down and all of your employees brought in for questioning." Sarah felt amazed at the threats she was throwing at Henry—weak threats, ones that she might never be able to follow through on, but threats he believed, nonetheless. She was crossing a very thin line, one good cops were not supposed to cross. But when she looked at Manford's scared face, she took another step over the line. "I'll have every person I know memorize your face, and they won't hesitate to beat you down, is that clear?"

Manford stared at Sarah. "Wow...you really do care about me," he whispered, feeling a powerful love erupt in his heart.

Amanda stepped into the kitchen, saw Sarah on the phone, and stopped. Sarah locked eyes with her. Amanda nodded her head, quickly made her way to Manford, and put a reassuring hand on his shoulder. "The threats end now, Mr. Billinger."

"The little rat is a liar!" Henry sputtered.

"No, Mr. Billinger, he is not. You are the liar. You are a conman and an abuser, and I won't let it continue." Sarah felt her temper continue to rise. She felt like a momma bear protecting her cub. "If Manford did rightfully steal from you, Mr. Billinger, you must file a report with your local authorities. You must present your case before a judge. If there is reasonable cause to extradite, your state will contact us, and I will personally fly Manford back to New York and hire the best lawyer money can buy. A lawyer who can talk about abuses of employment law, abuses of safety regulations, about wage theft. Would you like that? With a lawyer like that, at most, if Manford is found guilty, he might get a slap on the wrist. And you, Mr. Billinger, will pay heavy court fees and lawyer fees for that slap on the wrist. And then the law will come after you for every other evil deed you have tried to get away with." Sarah looked down at Manford. "If you want a fight, we are prepared to fight. But I assure you, Mr. Billinger, you will lose."

Henry saw nothing but red before his eyes. The cold rain, the jet, the terminal, the sounds of the airport, everything vanished. "No one speaks to me this way...do you hear me, woman? No one. You've just made yourself an enemy...do you hear me?" he hissed. "Henry Billinger loses to no one." And then Henry made a fatal mistake. "You're a dead woman, is that clear?"

Sarah opened her eyes. "And you, Mr. Billinger, have just threatened the wrong person," she said. "This conversation is being recorded and as soon as we hang up, every word you spoke is going to be sent to the FBI and the local authorities in your area."

The red before Henry's vision darkened. So what if the phone conversation was being recorded? So what if he was going to lose everything? Henry Billinger would not go down without ensuring his enemies were destroyed. But he had to play smart...real smart. "So be it," he said and ended the call, licked his cracked lips, and began scheming about his next step.

Sarah hung up the phone and looked down at Manford. "I just bluffed a moron," she said in a tired voice. "But I better turn that bluff into reality." She dialed Conrad. It was time to make sure a bully was chased out of the school yard; or so she hoped, for Manford's sake.

CHAPTER FIVE

Sarah drove Amanda's truck into Snow Falls instead of her jeep, mostly because her jeep was low on gas. The drive was silent. Manford was lost in his own thoughts and Sarah and Amanda didn't want to bother him. "Well, here we are," Sarah said, parking in front of the station. She spotted Conrad's truck and breathed a sigh of relief. Sure, Conrad was expecting her arrival, but deep down, Sarah always feared her husband would somehow...vanish, and be replaced by a horrible nightmare. "Let's go inside, huh?"

"Oh, I'm causing nothing but trouble," Manford told Sarah in a miserable voice. "Please, drive me to the nearest airport and let me fly to Mexico...or Australia."

"Buddy, you don't even have a passport," Sarah pointed out.

"Then...I'll fly to...Los Angeles and vanish. Henry won't be able to find me there...I'll blend in with the homeless population and—"

"No, you won't," Sarah told Manford in a stern voice. "Running isn't the answer, Manford. In life, you have to stand your ground and fight." Sarah nodded her head toward the front of the station. "Henry found you in Alaska and he'll find you in Los Angeles, if you run there. But at least here you have people who love you and who will stand by you."

"She's right, love," Amanda told Manford and gently rubbed his shoulder with a gloved hand. "There's been many times that I wanted to run away from my fears. But sometimes...you just have to stay and fight."

"And die," Manford added in a worried voice.

"Sometimes dying bravely is better than living as a coward, love," Amanda explained.

"Amanda is right, Manford. We have to fight against the darkness. All around us, darkness is spreading rapidly across the world...through people's hearts." Sarah put her arm around Manford. "You know, I'm pretty sure David was scared when he went up against Goliath."

"I know the story."

"We all do," Sarah nodded her head. "But do we really think about it? I mean, Goliath was this giant...and all of a sudden, here comes this little shepherd boy with a sling and a few rocks. Why, I bet Goliath had a good laugh, at least until he realized the Lord was with David."

"I...haven't read my Bible in a while, Sarah," Manford confessed. "What are you trying to say?"

"I'm trying to show you that it's not the size of your opponent that matters. It's the size of your faith...a faith that lives deep within our hearts and has nothing to do with the size of our enemy." Sarah squeezed Manford's shoulder. "Sometimes the bad guys win, but not forever. And sometimes the good guys win, but not every time. It's a constant fight between good and evil, Manford, and there are always bodies left lying on the battlefield. But if we give up, throw down our swords, and run away scared, then we let the evil win."

"Sarah, I'm a little person," Manford pointed out in a desperate voice. "A third-grader could beat the snot out of me. I'm no match for Henry Billinger. It's not about faith—"

"Maybe not just faith alone, love," Amanda cut in, "but remember, you're not walking alone anymore."

Manford looked up into Sarah's face, and then glanced over at Amanda. He saw two loving women who were willing to risk their lives for him. Shame and guilt quickly washed through his heart. "Two women willing to fight for me...and here I sit wanting to run," he said in an ashamed voice. "Yeah, my old man was right...Manford Sappers is a coward."

"You're not a coward," Sarah promised Manford.

"Sure, I am," Manford sighed. "I'm sitting between two women trying to figure out where I can run to. I always ran from Henry...but he knew me too well. He always used my mom to bring me back. When my old man died, that was the last defense...Henry really tore into me. He threatened to kill my mother if I ever ran off again." Manford felt anger and bitterness fill his heart. "When mom was diagnosed with cancer...the doctors didn't give her but a few months to live. Henry...fired her...wouldn't pay her the wages he owed...and forced me to keep working for him. He threatened to hurt mom if I didn't." Manford squeezed his hands together. "I...didn't steal mom's back pay from Henry...or not fully. He owed her maybe a couple hundred dollars, he never paid well. But I stole more than that...I stole a months' worth of profits. That's what I buried next to my mother's grave before I left New York...money that monster owed my mom...money she earned through her blood, sweat, and tears, and in the end...through her death. It was my final revenge." Manford looked up at Sarah. "After I buried the money, I bolted...and ended up here."

Sarah pulled Manford close. "It's okay," she tried to soothe him.

"I stole money...I'm a criminal. Henry has every right to —" Manford tried to tell Sarah.

"No. He has no right," Sarah said firmly. "Sometimes a broken, angry heart can make a man do things he later regrets," Sarah told Manford. "You are not a monster. Henry Billinger is the monster."

"But I broke the law," Manford insisted.

Sarah sighed. She looked to Amanda for help. Amanda simply patted Manford's shoulder. "You took money that you believe belonged to your mother. You were clearly both mistreated horribly at the hands of this Billinger fellow...I highly doubt he had detailed accounting books ready to prove anything. So until someone can prove to us that the money you took doesn't belong to your mother, well then, love, it's your word against the word of someone who sounds like a truly rotten egg."

Manford couldn't believe his ears. Why were Sarah and Amanda defending him after he openly admitted to stealing from Henry Billinger? He didn't have a clue. What he did know was that a light snow was beginning to fall, and he was feeling mighty scrunched up sitting in Amanda's truck. "I need some air."

"Of course," Sarah said and quickly climbed out of the driver's side and stepped into the lightly falling snow. As she did, Conrad stepped out of the station. He spotted Sarah and walked over to her. "Hey, honey," she said.

Conrad kissed Sarah on the cheek. "I called New York. Some good friends of mine are going to pay Billinger a visit. I also called a friend I know at the FBI. He's going to check into Billinger for us. Who knows, maybe we'll get a nibble?"

"We need to dig deep, Conrad," Sarah said and looked over at Manford, who climbed out of the truck and hurried over to Sarah and Conrad. "Conrad made a few calls, Manford. Some of New York's finest are going to start pushing in toward Henry Billinger. Who knows, maybe they'll find something useful?"

"I'm not so sure," Manford shook his head, feeling warm in the freezing cold instead of, well...freezing. "Henry is a clever, sneaky snake. He knows how to fix his books, bend the payroll, find tax loopholes, all sorts of stuff." Manford looked up and down the street, spotted cozy little shops blanketed in snow—unaware of the deadly killers that had tainted the street in the not-so-distant past—and sighed at its beauty. "It's sure pretty here. I really like it. Feels...clean."

"A lot different than New York, huh?" Conrad asked.

"And London," Amanda said, stepping up next to Manford.

Manford nodded his head. "I guess it is," he agreed. "The streets of New York always had a way of getting into my system. The subways...Times Square...all the cabs...the place kinda sucked me in. But it always felt...dirty, underneath, you know? Like there was something...something ugly underneath all the bright lights that could never quite get scrubbed clean, no matter how hard you tried. Mom never wanted to live in New York. Her family was from Phoenix...she missed the desert." Manford shook his head. "I'm not much of a desert person, but I understood why mom wanted to go home."

Conrad reached out and patted Manford's shoulder. "Let's go inside and get some coffee, huh?"

"Nah," Manford said. "I think I want to see Sarah's coffee shop. No sense in letting Henry spoil this day. It's not like he's going to appear out of nowhere, right?" Manford walked his eyes around the snowy town. "My old man could be a real coward...a drunkard, cruel to me and my mom...but he sure stood to attention when Henry was in the room. He thought the sun rose and set in Henry's pocket. I don't want to be like my old man, not anymore. I guess if Henry shows up...he shows up."

Sarah glanced down and looked Manford in his eyes. "Courage begins exactly like that. It begins here," she said and touched his heart through his thick, warm jacket with one gloved finger. "You're scared right now, but I promise, when the time arrives—if the time ever arrives— you'll find the courage you need, the same courage David had."

Manford stared into Sarah's eyes and felt a strange, if not amazing, feeling enter his heart. What was the feeling? Was it...hope? Yes, the feeling was hope; actual hope. "I don't want to be a coward anymore."

"You're not a coward." Sarah smiled and kissed Manford's cold cheek. "You never were. If you were, you wouldn't be standing here. You would have already made tracks out of town."

Manford seemed startled. "Do you really think so?"

Sarah smiled and touched the coat Amanda had bought him once again. "You're not wearing your street clothes, are you? You ate my breakfast...slept a good night's sleep...did some honest work. I don't think that looks like cowardice to me."

Manford glanced down at his new coat. "Hey...maybe you're right," he said in a proud voice. "I guess...deep down, I'm still pretty scared...but I'm also not running. That's gotta be worth something, right?"

"It sure is," Conrad said in a proud voice. "You're—" he began to say but stopped abruptly when a red BMW sped up to the station and skidded to a stop, nearly colliding with Amanda's truck. A blonde woman in her early thirties stormed out of the BMW wearing a flashy white leather jacket and marched up to Conrad. "Ms. Appleson," he said.

Sarah turned her eyes to Macy Appleson. What she saw

was a woman who had dyed her hair blonde, purchased a face designed by plastic surgeons, and wore a wardrobe that made her look like a silly twit. She saw a plastic person who possessed no heart and no soul. "Detective Spencer, I demand to know how my mother's case is progressing," Macy demanded with a shake of her carefully coiffed hair. She looked spoiled, from her flawless makeup all the way down to the tips of her impractical high-heeled boots.

Manford studied Macy warily. Sure, he thought, the dame was good-looking—at least on the outside—but she looked like the type he knew from the city: the kind with a grimy soul hidden on the inside. He knew Macy's kind. He knew women like Macy loved dollar bills and would marry any man who offered a pile of cash. Money was Macy's true love.

"A murder case takes time," Conrad said in a calm voice.

"My mother was murdered," Macy snapped and raised a finger at Conrad. "I want answers, not excuses."

Sarah felt her cheeks turn red and she started to open her mouth to tell off the young woman, but Conrad quickly shook his head to stop her. The last thing in the world he wanted his wife to do was slug a spoiled brat who was already making his life difficult. "Ms. Appleson, I've explained to you that the system is still down. We're not able to network with any outside agencies at the moment. I'm afraid that until we can do that, your mother's body will have to remain at the hospital until an official autopsy can be conducted."

Macy narrowed her eyes. "I'll sue this town for every penny it's worth if my mother's body remains in that hick hospital for one more second."

"I look forward to seeing the lawsuit," Conrad told Macy, keeping his voice easy. "If you have the money to hire a lawyer, sue until you're blue in the face. It won't change the fact that the system is down, and we can't network with outside sources."

Macy's face turned red. "I want answers," she snapped. "I want to know who killed my mother."

"So do I," Conrad nodded his head. "But answers take time."

Macy stomped her shiny boot heel into the snow. "I don't have time. I have to be back in Los Angeles for an audition in less than a week, do you hear me?"

"Don't hold your breath," Conrad replied, making Sarah and Amanda hide grins behind their hands.

"Oh, you two think my mother's death is funny, do you?" Macy growled. "Well let me tell you, my mother was a fine woman, and I'm not going to rest until her killer is behind bars."

Manford studied Macy's eyes as she snapped at Sarah and Amanda. Something in the woman's eyes didn't sit well with him. The woman gave him a bad feeling—a really bad feeling.

"I'll be in touch," Conrad told Macy and pointed at her BMW. "We don't allow double parking. Move your car."

Macy's cheeks turned pink and it looked like steam might rise from her head in a moment. "I better hear from you soon," she ordered Conrad. Macy stormed back to her BMW and drove away, the tires kicking up snow as she skidded out into the street.

"My, what a piece of work," Amanda said in a disgusted voice.

Sarah watched Macy drive away down the snowy street. "She's smaller than I thought," she told Conrad.

"Mrs. Appleson had some pounds on her," Conrad nodded her head.

"What are you two getting at?" Amanda asked and then caught on. "Oh, you think that brat was too weak to strangle her mother?"

"She's a smart cookie," Sarah told Conrad.

Conrad rubbed his chin. "I'm thinking Macy Appleson hired someone to murder her mother," he said in a thoughtful voice. "The only problem is the killer could be miles away by now. I have zero evidence to go off of until the system comes back up."

"Why not have your friends in New York help you?" Manford asked.

"I've already loaded them down with tracking Billinger down," Conrad explained. "I don't like to press my friendship too hard."

Manford shrugged his shoulders. "Real friends don't mind being pressed." He pointed at Sarah and Amanda. "Real friends stand by you. That's what you guys are teaching me, anyway."

Conrad looked down at Manford and smiled. "You're right, Manford," he said. "I guess I can ask...let's see...maybe Matthew Conyers can look into Mrs. Appleson's will for me."

"Wouldn't hurt," Manford agreed, even though he had no idea who Matthew Conyers was.

"I'll go inside and make some calls." Conrad patted Manford's shoulder, kissed Sarah's cheek, stuck his tongue out at Amanda, and walked back inside the station. As he did, Amanda made a quick snowball and decked him in the back of the head. "You still lost at Scrabble!" he yelled behind him.

"That's because you cheated!" Amanda yelled back. Conrad threw his hands at Amanda and vanished into the station.

"You two," Sarah shook her head. "Manford, want to see my coffee shop?"

"Sure, why not."

Sarah nodded her head down the street. "This way," she said and began walking.

Manford looked over his shoulder at Amanda. "You coming?"

"Sure am," Amanda smiled. She grabbed Manford's hand and began walking behind Sarah. "I have a handsome man at my side, a lovely winter day to bask in, and a dear friend to confide all of my deepest secrets to. Oh, what beauty," she sighed in a silly, dramatic voice.

Manford felt a smile touch his lips. Sure, danger was on its way to Snow Falls—he felt the danger deep inside of his heart—but so what? For the moment, things were...well, cool. Why stress over a fight before the first punch is thrown? "I just hope I don't prove a coward when the first punch really is thrown," he thought, as the image of a deadly lion ghosted through his worried mind.

Manford sure liked Sarah's coffee shop. He liked the vintage design, too. The front room made him feel like he had walked back into the nineteen-thirties; into a time that was simple, clean and good to live in. "Nice place," he told Sarah.

"It would be if I could ever stay open for business," Sarah replied. "I manage to open up for business two or three days a week. Lately it's been two."

"How do you make money?" Manford asked.

"Money isn't really my objective." Sarah glanced at Amanda. Amanda smiled and wandered back to the kitchen. She returned a few minutes later with a plate full of homemade cinnamon rolls. "Coffee is brewing," she announced, set the plate of cinnamon rolls down on a table, and looked at Manford. "Sarah and I love this place," she explained. "It's a labor of love, especially in a tiny town like Snow Falls. We don't worry about profits."

"Never heard of a person running a business just for fun," Manford said, shrugged his shoulders, and wandered up to the front counter and studied a glass cake display. It was bare. "No cake?"

"Amanda baked a Snow Cake," Sarah told Manford. "Unfortunately, she ate what was left of it."

Amanda winked at Manford. "I sure did."

"What's a Snow Cake?" Manford asked.

"A chocolate cake dusted with powdered sugar and frosted with a yummy cream cheese," Amanda beamed. "My own personal creation."

"In other words, it's a sugar cake," Sarah teased.

"You bet," Amanda agreed.

Manford imagined Amanda's cake in his mind. The cake sounded good...with a cup of coffee, that was. "So, what now?" he asked.

"O'Mally's?" Amanda asked in an excited voice. "While I was buying short stuff some clothes, I saw this beautiful blouse that was on sale. I would have bought it, but I was in a hurry. And you know me, love, I don't like to buy and run. Shopping is an art form."

"With you, shopping is more than an art form," Sarah teased Amanda. She looked at Manford. "You do need more clothes."

"I guess I do," Manford agreed. "But I want to earn my clothes. I'll do chores. I'll shovel out your jeep and Conrad's truck each morning until the snow melts...and take Mittens for her walks and carry in wood and wash the dishes and wash the clothes and—"

"Oh, please oh please, come live at my cabin," Amanda begged Manford. "Oh please, love, come live at my cabin."

Sarah rolled her eyes. "We'll discuss your chore list," she told Manford and pointed to the front door. "Come on, we better get going before Amanda drops to her knees and begins begging."

Amanda winked at Manford and walked back outside. Manford grinned, followed Amanda, and made his way back toward her truck. Ten minutes later, he walked through the front glass doors of O'Mally's as a customer rather than a thief. The store was warm, cozy, and, to his relief, not very busy. A few shoppers, mostly older women, were out and about, pushing their shopping carts at a snail's pace, looking at this or that, in no hurry to buy or leave.

"Maybe we should get a cup of coffee before we start shopping?" Amanda asked and rubbed her nose. "The wind and snow is really picking up again, and I caught a chill walking in from the parking lot."

Manford glanced toward the snack bar and spotted Amy Huntsdale standing behind the snack counter. "Oh man," he groaned, "that pretty face is going to think the worst of me."

Sarah followed Manford's eyes, saw Amy, and understood Manford's worry. After all, she reminded herself, Amy had watched Conrad slap a pair of handcuffs on Manford and haul him away last time. "Uh...stay here," she said in a quick voice and hurried away toward the snack bar.

"What's she doing?" Manford asked Amanda in a worried voice. Amanda shrugged her shoulders. Her mind was now on the blouse she had seen the day before. Manford shoved his hands into the pockets of his coat, not realizing he was still wearing his earmuffs, and watched Sarah approach Amy. "Oh man," he moaned and began shifting from one nervous foot to another. He watched Sarah begin talking with Amy and then, to his horror, saw Amy look past Sarah's shoulder, right at him. "Oh man..." he said and moved behind Amanda. A couple of minutes later, Sarah waved a hand in his direction. "What did you do?" he asked in a miserable voice.

"Huh?" Amanda asked. Her eyes were locked in the direction the blouse was located. "What did you say, love?"

"Come on, you two!" Sarah called out.

"Oh man," Manford groaned and nervously walked to the snack bar with Amanda. When he reached the snack counter, he saw Amy toss a beautiful smile at him. "Uh...hi...about yesterday—"

"Sarah explained," Amy smiled. "No worries, okay? Now, what will you have to eat?" she asked and looked at Amanda with nervous eyes. Amanda focused on the photo of a kosher chili dog on the menu board. "We're...still kinda low on kosher dogs, okay?"

Sarah grinned. "I'll have a coffee and a hot pretzel." Sarah looked at Manford. "What will you have?"

"Uh...coffee and...uh...a cheeseburger," Manford blushed.

"Four chili dogs, fries, hot pretzel and coffee for me, love," Amanda told Amy in a happy voice. "This English Muffin has some shopping to do and she's going to need her strength."

Sarah rolled her eyes and then laughed. "Manford, will you bring our order to the table?" she asked and dragged Amanda off to a booth.

"And take off your earmuffs," Amanda called out as Sarah pulled her away.

"Earmuffs..." Manford threw his hands up to his head, felt his earmuffs, and then blushed. "Oh...yeah."

"You can take off your gloves, too," Amy smiled.

Manford turned red. "Uh...yeah...guess I should."

Amy giggled. "You're...um, you're really cute," she said.

Manford's face turned even redder. No woman had ever called him cute before. The feeling was...great! "I...uh...I'm Manford Sappers...uh...what's your name?"

Amy touched her name tag. "Amy."

"Oh...yeah, of course," Manford said, feeling like a complete idiot. "Uh...I guess we better pay, huh?"

"Oh, I never ring up the bill until Amanda is through eating. She makes several orders and if I ring up the bill the first time, I'll have to change it three times by the time Amanda finishes eating me out of house and home." Amy smiled at Manford. "Amanda is a really great person. I really like her. I really like Sarah, too. You're lucky to be with them. Those two women have always treated me with a lot of kindness...a lot more than I can say for the folks I knew back in Maryland."

"You're not from Snow Falls?"

Amy shook her head. "My parents divorced when I was fourteen. I lived with my dad in Maryland. It wasn't...easy. He liked his beers. We ended up living in a rough neighborhood...lots of violence. I was in a really bad school and nobody ever stops to think what it's like, you know? Trying to go from your awful trailer home to your awful school...everyone's so judgmental..." Amy stopped, wiping her hands on a towel. "Oh, I'm sorry. I didn't mean to talk too much."

"You're not talking too much," Manford promised Amy. "I'm just...well, kinda surprised. Your life sounds a little similar to mine."

"Really?"

Manford sighed. "My dad was a drinker, too. I've had...a rough life." He stopped, not wanting to overwhelm her, but feeling a budding sympathy between them. "You want to talk about judgmental? I usually assume girls like you are just making fun of me when they talk to me."

"Why?"

"Look at my size."

"So?" Amy asked.

"I'm a little person. Doesn't that bother you?"

Amy shook her head. "I've seen guys who are tall and built like bears who are shorter than you are inside their hearts." Amy looked Manford in his nervous eyes, feeling very nervous herself. "My granny died when I was twelve years old. Before she died, she always taught me that a person should be seen for who they are inside of their hearts, not what they look like on the outside."

Manford scuffed one boot against the floor, looking away. "You wouldn't like my heart...I haven't exactly lived an honest life."

"Neither have I," Amy whispered. "Can you keep a secret?"

Manford looked up into Amy's sweet eyes. "A secret?"

Amy nodded her head. "I have an arrest record."

"You do?" Manford asked in a shocked voice.

"Back in Maryland, when I was in high school, I hung out with the wrong group of girls...girls who liked to steal things...a lot." Amy glanced at Sarah. "I started stealing, too...mostly because I was really angry at my dad. I wasn't very good at it, though. I was arrested a couple times. Juvenile stuff. Finally, this one judge, a real hard case, told me if he ever saw my face back in his courtroom, he was going to send me to prison." Amy sighed. "I went to live with my brother in New York state after that. I...really didn't want to speak to my mom at the time. I kinda blamed her for the divorce. Anyway, things kept going downhill for me and finally I called my mom here in Snow Falls and she asked me to come live with her. So please don't think I'm some kind of princess, Manford." Amy sighed. "I'm a twenty-one-year-old making fries and chili dogs in rural Alaska...I'm a real winner, huh?"

Manford saw sadness replace Amy's sweet smile. His heart broke. "I have an arrest record, too," he confessed. "You shouldn't be ashamed. Life is hard, and people don't understand what it's like. I did some shoplifting in my time, you know. I...grew up in a circus...my old man was rough. I kept hitting the streets, trying to be tough...stealing...doing other bad stuff. I didn't even go to school most of the time. My mom taught me to read and write and do some basic math. About all I know how to do is drive a clown car, get hit in the face with a pie, sweep up elephant dung and take down tents."

Amy stared into Manford's eyes and saw a heart that had been broken down by life—a heart that was a stranger to romantic love. She saw a heart that had never even experienced a first kiss, understood what it felt like to hold a woman's hand, take a walk together on the beach— she saw a heart that understood only loneliness and bitterness, pain and fear. Manford reminded Amy a lot of herself. "I think you're right. We're a lot alike," she said in a soft voice. "You and me, we're a pair, huh?"

Manford kicked at the floor again. "Only difference is someday your white knight in shining armor is going to save you...I'm never going to be a knight in shining armor for any girl."

Amy sighed. "Manford, don't say that," she begged. "Don't put yourself down. I meant it when I said you're cute. You're very handsome. I thought that yesterday when I saw you."

"You did?" Manford asked in shock.

"Yes," Amy blushed.

"Even though I'm a...little person?"

"You keep saying that like it means something. Height has nothing to do with it," Amy said. "Manford, we're all human...only separated by ugly ideas about what society thinks is beautiful or normal or whatever." Amy sighed. "Luckily, my granny raised me on the Bible and lately I've been reading the Bible again."

"What is the Bible teaching you?"

"That the Lord will show us what's right and what's wrong," Amy replied, and her sweet smile came back to her face. "And what's right is looking at a person's heart, not their height."

When she said those words, her clear blue eyes looking right into his own, Manford felt a strange little skip of his heart. Like something in his soul responded to her. He liked the feeling.

"Are you two going to talk all day? I'm hungry!" Amanda yelled. "The grill's hot by now, love."

Amy sighed. "I better get to work. It's been really nice talking to you."

"Uh...maybe we can talk again?" Manford asked.

"I would like that," Amy told Manford and blushed. She sure liked Manford. Not only was he handsome, he made her feel...what was the word...safe. Yes, safe. Why? Amy had no idea.

"Uh...be right back," Manford told Amy and rushed off to the booth Sarah and Amanda were sitting in. He tossed down his gloves and earmuffs and nervously looked over his shoulder. "Uh...Sarah?"

"The answer is yes," Sarah beamed. "You can invite Amy over for dinner tonight."

"How in the world did you know what I was going to ask?" Manford said, flabbergasted.

Sarah and Amanda both giggled. "All a woman has to do is read your face, love," Amanda told Manford. "Now, get back over there, you little stud, and ask that sweet young lady to dinner."

"I...uh..." Manford stuttered. "I've never asked a girl out on a date before. What do I say? What do I do? What if I—"

Sarah reached out and took Manford's hand. "Treat Amy with love and care and everything will be fine," she promised.

"But..." Manford hesitated. Suddenly, his mind saw Henry Billinger's creepy, deadly face appear. "But Henry Billinger...I know he's going to show up here sooner or later. Maybe I shouldn't, huh? I mean, what if something happens?"

"Stop letting fear control you, honey," Sarah whispered and nodded her head at Amy. "Draw your sword and fight."

"A little person with a sword. That's a laugh."

Sarah touched Manford's hand. "A man with a sword. Height doesn't define a man, his heart does."

"That's what...Amy was kinda telling me," Manford told Sarah.

"That's because Amy is a very smart young lady, love," Amanda smiled. "Now, go ask her to dinner before some other bloke does, okay?"

Manford looked into Sarah's and Amanda's eyes, saw complete love staring back at him, and smiled. "Okay," he said, drew in a shaky breath, and walked back to the snack counter on nervous legs only a woman could give a man. "Uh...Amy?"

"Yes?" Amy asked, feeling her stomach tighten.

"I was thinking...maybe you might like to...uh...come over...for uh...dinner tonight? You see, I'm living with Sarah now and...she said it would be cool," Manford asked in a voice that trembled on almost every word.

"Oh, that would be great," Amy smiled, hiding her elation. "What time?"

"What time?" Manford asked. "Oh...I didn't ask that."

"Six o'clock," Sarah called out. "We're having pizza."

Amy giggled. "Six o'clock and pizza it is."

"Really?" Manford asked, unable to believe that a beautiful woman like Amy was agreeing to have dinner with him. "You mean it? You'll really come for dinner?"

"Uh huh," Amy nodded her head and blushed all over. "I would love to have dinner with you, Manford. I really do think you're very handsome...and very sweet. I think we have a lot to talk about."

Manford stood in shock, and then he did what any guy would do: he smiled, blushed, and hurried away. "She said yes!" he called out to Sarah and Amanda in a voice filled with absolute happiness.

But what Manford didn't know was that as he ran back to

the booth Sarah and Amanda were sitting in...Henry Billinger was boarding his flight.

"Time to die, you little rat," Henry hissed under his breath. "And I'll be sure to make Detective Sarah Spencer suffer, too. Oh yes, she'll suffer. No one talks to Henry Billinger the way she did and lives."

CHAPTER SIX

M anford looked up at Sarah with nervous eyes. "I don't look too goofy, do I?" he asked as Sarah folded down the collar on his white shirt over the crew neck of a gray sweater.

"You look handsome," Sarah smiled. "And that cologne...Amy is going to melt in your arms."

Manford blushed, glanced down at the fancy black loafers on his feet, and then looked up into Sarah's warm face. "I...thanks, you know? This life is all new to me, Sarah, but you gotta know that I'm grateful. Honest, I am."

Sarah bent down and put her hands on Manford's shoulders. "I know you are. I saw goodness in you the very first time my eyes saw you. I know you have a good, decent heart."

"I'm supposed to be a loner...real tough guy, you know?"

"It's tougher to love than to be alone," Sarah explained. "Now, Conrad should be here with Amy at any minute. So why don't you and I go out to the kitchen and make sure Amanda hasn't eaten up all the pizza?"

"I guess we better," Manford smiled. "But before we do..." Manford hurried away to his bed, reached under the mattress, and pulled out a small box.

"What is that?" Sarah asked.

Manford stared down at the small red and white box in his hands. "It's not much. You see, Conrad gave me twenty dollars for helping him shovel out his truck...and I kinda wanted to get you something for being so kind to me."

"Oh, Manford, you didn't have to—"

"I know I didn't have to," Manford politely interrupted, "but...well, the twenty dollars Conrad gave me was honest money...clean money. I wanted to buy you a present with the first clean money I earned."

Sarah almost started to cry. "I'm very honored."

Manford drew in a deep breath, walked back to Sarah on nervous legs, and handed her the present. "The present is really for Amanda, too...but I wanted you to open it first."

"Okay," Sarah smiled and, with happy hands, opened the

small box. A simple silver key sat in the box. "I'm afraid...I don't understand. What is it for?"

"The key," Manford explained, "is to me. Because I...don't ever want to lock you out." Manford ran back to his bed, picked up his pillow, and pulled out an old silver key and held it up. "My mother gave me this key when I was a little boy. She said as long as I had this key...I had her heart." Manford felt a tear leave his eye. "As long as you have that key...you, Amanda and Conrad...you guys will be in my heart."

Sarah couldn't stand it. She felt tears begin falling from her eyes. "I'm very honored," she told Manford, walked over to him, and hugged him in a way only a mother could. "You have my heart, too."

"I know," Manford said, hugging Sarah back. He wiped at his tears. "I guess we need to go check on Amanda, huh?"

"I guess we should," Sarah laughed and wiped at her own tears. Manford nodded his head, put his key back under the pillow on his bed, and walked to the kitchen with Sarah at his side. He spotted Amanda trying to steal a slice of cheese pizza.

"June Bug!" Sarah yelled.

Amanda nearly jumped out of her skin. "What? I was...just sampling a piece..."

Sarah grinned. "Sure, you were."

Amanda touched her heart and fanned her face. "You nearly scared ten years out of me...and I'm only twenty," she said and winked at Manford. Manford winked back.

"If you're twenty, I'm twenty-one," Sarah told Amanda and hurried to check the three pizza boxes sitting on the kitchen counter. Three two-liter bottles of root beer were sitting next to the pizza boxes along with a plate of homemade brownies. "Well, everything looks good," she said and glanced at the back door. "Conrad should be here at any minute—" before Sarah could finish her sentence, she heard Conrad's truck arrive. "Ah, there he is now."

Manford felt his hands turn sweaty. Amanda smiled, handed him a brown napkin, and told him to put the napkin in his pocket. "When my son went on his first date, he sweated enough to fill an ocean," she said. "Anytime you need to, just reach down into your pocket and wipe your palms off, okay?"

"Thanks, Amanda," Manford replied in a grateful voice. "You sure are great."

"Did you hear that?" Amanda asked Sarah. "I'm great."

"And you have a little pizza sauce on the side of your mouth," Sarah told her best friend and winked at her.

"Oh, you," Amanda laughed and wiped at the pizza sauce with her hand.

Sarah giggled. "What are sisters for?" she asked and hurried to the back door, opened it, and looked out into a dark night filled with icy winds whipping up at a sky glittering with stars. The snow had passed—for the time being—allowing Snow Falls a chance to breathe before the next storm arrived. "Here they come," she called out, spotting Conrad helping a lovely young woman wearing a black coat walk through the snow.

"Oh man," Manford groaned quietly.

"You'll be fine, handsome," Amanda promised and then clapped her hands. "Oh, this is going to be so great. I bet they're going to end up getting married," she told Sarah.

"Married?" Manford gulped.

Sarah grinned. "Maybe," she agreed and moved away from the back door. "Hurry inside and get warm," she called out. "It's freezing out there."

Conrad burst through the back door with Amy, closed the back door, stomped snow off his boots, and then kissed Sarah on her cheek. "Smells like a pizza parlor in here."

Amy saw Manford, smiled, and then said hello to Sarah and Amanda. "It's nice of you to have me over for dinner."

"A pizza party," Amanda explained in an excited voice. She rushed over to Amy and removed the black coat she was wearing. "Oh, what a lovely blue dress. Where did you get it?" she gasped. "I want one."

"Uh...O'Mally's," Amy blushed. "It was on clearance."

Amanda hung up Amy's coat. "I went through the clearance rack with a fine-toothed comb and didn't see this dress," she complained.

Sarah sighed. "Please don't get her started," she begged Amy. "Coffee, honey?"

"Uh...yes, please," Amy smiled.

Conrad focused on Manford. The guy was standing like a block of stone, eyes fixed on the beautiful Amy. "I'll be back in a second, Sarah. I need to...uh...check on something. Manford, you can help me," he said, rushed over to Manford, grabbed his right hand, and hurried them out of the kitchen.

"What do you need help with?" Manford asked, walking into the living room with Conrad.

Conrad quickly bent down and put his hands on Manford's shoulders. "Okay, it's time for some guy-to-guy stuff," he explained.

"Guy-to-guy stuff?"

Conrad nodded his head. "Look, Manford, Amy is a

pretty girl who seems to like you. You need to relax and just be yourself, okay? If you stand around like a frozen stiff all night, you might run her off."

"I...don't know what to say to her," Manford confessed. "Conrad, you're...cool. Tell me what to do?"

"First and foremost," Conrad said, lowering his voice down to a whisper, "treat Amy with care and respect. Second, just be yourself and watch your mouth...no crude stuff, okay?" Manford nodded his head. "And third, don't try to act cool."

"But you're cool," Manford insisted.

"I'm a dopey cop who doesn't have enough sense to get a real job," Conrad told Manford. "I make lousy money, nearly been killed more times than I can remember, and have a gut carved out of bad coffee and stale donuts."

"But Sarah loves you—"

"And I love Sarah," Conrad told Manford. "But our love came over time, Manford. You see, Sarah and I bonded while going through a lot of dangerous stuff. I didn't have time to play it cool...I was too busy keeping my head down," Conrad patted Manford's shoulder. "Look, just be yourself and let time take its course. Don't be in a rush to find the perfect love song and all of that stuff...just...be a friend and then, if love comes...hey, it comes."

Manford stared into Conrad's eyes. He had never had a

talk like this before. His father's version of talk had involved an open hand, if he was lucky, and a closed fist if he wasn't. "Thanks, Conrad. You're okay."

"So are you," Conrad smiled and walked Manford back into the kitchen. "Okay, when's dinner? I'm starved."

Amy smiled at Manford. "How has your day been going?" she asked.

Manford looked at Conrad. Conrad tossed him a wink. "Well," he told Amy and gestured at the clothes he was wearing, "Sarah and Amanda dressed me up like a doll, splashed me in cologne, and put new shoes on my feet," he told Amy and let a relieved smile spread across his face. "Now they're hoping I might ask you to marry me before dinner is over, but Conrad told me that we should be friends first."

"Spoilsport...party pooper," Amanda fussed at Conrad. "Sarah and I want a wedding!"

"Maybe Manford and Amy might want to decide that...at a later date...a faraway later date," Conrad told Amanda.

Amy blushed. "Uh...okay. Want to sit down?"

"Sure." Manford walked Amy to the kitchen table, pulled out a chair for her, and then went to his own chair. Sarah smiled and poured Manford and Amy a cup of coffee. She walked the two cups of coffee over to the table and sat them down. "I think we'll all have a cup of coffee before dinner, chat a little, and work up an appetite."

"Chat a little?" Conrad moaned.

"Yes, chat a little," Amanda said and shot Conrad an *I'll kill you if you ruin this night* look. Conrad winced. "Sure...chat a little," he said and hurried to pour himself a cup of coffee. As he did, the telephone rang. "I'll get it."

Manford tensed up. He watched Conrad answer the phone, expecting Henry Billinger to be on the other end. When Conrad began speaking to one of his friends from New York, he tried to relax. But when Conrad's face grew serious, his stomach tightened up again. "Uh oh," he whispered.

"What flight did he get on, Matthew?...I see. What about the circus?...I see," he said, giving Sarah a significant look across the room, "the Feds were already looking in his direction for smuggling illegal aliens in to work for him?...No, no, you've been a great help. Yeah, Sarah is fine. She's standing right here...no, no golf courses in Snow Falls yet, sorry...yeah...okay, Matt, thanks for all your help. Get up this way and pay me a visit, okay? Sure...okay, bye." Conrad hung up the phone and looked at Sarah with worried eyes. "Let's go talk in the living room, okay?"

"Is anything the matter?" Amy asked. "What's this all about?"

Before Conrad could give a polite answer, Manford began speaking. "Something is most definitely the matter," he told Amy, "and it's a little more than petty thievery, I'm afraid." To everyone's surprise, he began telling her all about Henry Billinger. When he finished speaking, he saw anger grip Amy's cheeks.

"Why, that awful man," Amy fumed. "Who does he think he is, bullying you around?" Amy looked at Conrad. "Detective Spencer, you have to do something!"

Conrad leaned against the back door. "Not much I can do until the guy arrives in town," he told Amy in a regretful voice. "My friend Matt told me Henry Billinger hopped a flight to Anchorage this afternoon." Conrad looked at Sarah. "The Feds were giving him a good eye. I guess it was just a matter of time before they moved in on him."

"The Feds...you mean the FBI...was really peeking into the circus tent?" Manford asked in a shocked voice. "I thought...all cops were crooked...especially the FBI. I mean, I heard stories about how the FBI played footsie with the mafia families in New York...lots of stuff like that."

"There are lots of rotten apples out there, Manford," Conrad said. "There are also lots of good apples out there. The NYPD is filled with good cops if you know where to look. The FBI isn't any different."

"Well...we just can't sit here and wait for that mean man to arrive and hurt Manford," Amy insisted.

Sarah saw fire enter Amy's eyes. It was good—really good —to see life waking up in the young woman. "Amy is right," she said and softly patted Amy's shoulder and calmly walked away to pour herself a cup of coffee. "But Conrad is also right," she added. "Right now, there isn't much we can do except wait."

"I'll call Andrew and have him tell all of our guys to keep an eye out," Conrad told Sarah. "I would call Anchorage, but there's not much I can do with the system still down... stupid hackers. The old days were much better. All of these computer systems...networks...databases...it's just a train wreck waiting to happen. At least in the old days I could pull a hard copy out of a file drawer."

"In the old days, a person like Henry Billinger wouldn't have been allowed to get as far as he has," Sarah added. "In the old days, people respected truth. We didn't need computers and miles of red tape to work through."

"That's true, love," Amanda sighed. "In the thirties, people respected the law and the law respected the people. Now it's a whole us-versus-them mentality that is killing everybody's integrity." Amanda walked over to Manford and rubbed his shoulder. "In today's times, more and more monsters are appearing because society is decaying into a kind of darkness that only monsters can live in."

Manford looked up at Amanda, saw a flash of nightmares run across her eyes, and—instead of feeling fear—felt anger grip his chest. "It's not fair," he said and hit the table. Both Amanda and Amy jumped. "I'm supposed to be on my very first date...and Henry is ruining everything! He's always ruined everything. I'm..." Manford jumped down from his chair and began walking around the kitchen. "What right does he have to control me? I'm a free man...I deserve...what my mother deserved...what she never got...to be free. To be happy."

"That's it," Sarah told Manford, "get mad...get so mad that you're willing to fight instead of remain scared."

Manford looked at Sarah. "I am mad...I'm really mad. I'm also still very...scared." Manford looked at Amy with shame in his eyes. "Henry Billinger once told me that if I ever betrayed him, he would feed me to his lions. My old man...was killed by his lions. The cops ruled his death accidental, but I know it was Henry...that monster let his lions loose on my old man when he was too drunk to move..."

Amy stood up, walked over to Manford, and gently took his hand. "Manford?"

Manford looked up into the prettiest eyes he had ever seen. "Yeah?"

"No one is ever going to feed you to any lions," Amy

promised. "I know I'm not the world's greatest person, but I promise I'll stand by you, okay?"

Manford couldn't believe his ears. Why was a pretty girl like Amy promising to stand by him? Snow Falls, Alaska sure was a strange—and deadly—little town.

———

Conrad reached for a slice of pizza but stopped when the telephone rang again. "What now?" he asked and answered the call. "Yeah, Spencer speaking."

"Conrad, you better get over to Mrs. Appleson's cabin," Andrew said in a serious cop voice. He threw his gaze around a warm living room decorated with lovely furnishings and more candles than he could count. Macy Appleson was in the middle of the living room, lying face down on a dark green carpet. "Macy Appleson has been strangled to death."

"Oh man," Conrad griped. "I knew she wasn't working alone. This is awful."

"Looks like you were right," Andrew nodded his head. "Mrs. Appleson's neighbor, Joan Tucker, called me and reported a strange black truck she had seen driving away from Mrs. Appleson's cabin. I tried to call Macy Appleson, and when she didn't answer I decided to investigate."

Conrad ran his hand through his hair. "I'm on my way, Andrew," he said and then quickly added: "Did the killer make it seem like there was a burglary?"

"Not as far as I can see. Everything in the cabin looks in order."

"Okay...give me twenty minutes." Conrad hung up the phone. "I have to go."

"What's the matter?" Amy asked. "What...killer? Does this have to do with Mrs. Appleson? I heard all about her death. I thought she just died, though."

Conrad grabbed his leather jacket off the coat rack. "I'm afraid it was more than that," he said and looked at Sarah. "You're going to have to drive Amy home. Just be careful, okay?"

Sarah hurried to the kitchen counter, grabbed two slices of pizza, and handed them to Conrad. "Eat on your way," she pleaded.

Conrad kissed Sarah's cheek and took the two slices of pizza. "I will," he promised and threw a quick eye at Manford. "Monsters are everyone, Manford. Henry Billinger isn't the only one. But if we give up the fight, we let them win."

Manford watched a brave man open the back door. "I'll fight," he promised. "I'll be just like you, Conrad."

"Not like me," Conrad corrected Manford as a gust of icy wind struck his face, "like yourself. Every hero is different, and every battle is different." Conrad quickly kissed Sarah's cheeks again and hurried out into the freezing night.

Sarah watched her husband vanish into the darkness, sighed, and closed the back door. "Pizza anyone?" she asked, feeling the festive mood dive down into a dark hole.

"Not really hungry," Manford said.

"Me, neither," Amy agreed.

"No sense in being worried on an empty stomach," Amanda pointed out. She grabbed a slice of cheese pizza, whispered a prayer of thanks, and dug in. "So what's the plan?" she asked Sarah while chewing her pizza. "Surely we're not going to wait for that fat rat to show up and start chasing poor Manford around town."

"I'm not sure," Sarah answered. She walked over to the kitchen table and sat down. "Unfortunately, there's not a whole lot we can do right now except...wait."

Amanda gobbled down her pizza and grabbed a second slice. "If that fat rat has your home phone number, I bet he can find your cabin," she told Sarah. "I think we should all relocate to my cabin."

"Isn't that...running?" Manford asked.

"Being safe doesn't mean you're being cowardly, love. We can pick our battlefield."

Sarah sipped at her coffee. "I need to call the Anchorage airport and see what flights from New York arrive today and what times."

"Now we're talking," Amanda said in a proud voice.

Amy looked at Manford. "I don't blame you for being scared. Honestly, I don't."

Manford didn't want to be scared. He was mad, angry and very upset—but yeah, fear hid deep down inside, and he couldn't quite shake it. But as he looked into Amy's eyes, a strange thought occurred to him, a thought he never thought he would have in a million years: what if he was worthy of asking Amy to be his wife, one day, when this was all over? What if they had children? It made him wonder what he would do if Henry Billinger was out to harm his own family: would he run? "No," Manford whispered, "I'll protect my family the way a man should."

"What?" Amy asked.

Manford looked deep into Amy's eyes. "Amy, the time for being scared is over. I have to stand my ground and fight. If I don't...I'll never stop being scared...inside." Manford walked his eyes over to Sarah. "Henry Billinger is just one person, Sarah...he's not invincible...he's just a slimy rat that needs to be cut down to size."

Sarah agreed. "I'll call the Anchorage airport and see what I can find out."

"Good idea," Manford said, feeling like a man preparing for battle.

Sarah stood up, walked to the telephone, and called information. She asked for the airport in Anchorage. A few minutes later, after waiting on hold, she finally began speaking to someone at the airport. "Okay...thanks. Now, can you connect me to airport security, please?" Sarah looked at Amanda and then over to the kitchen table. "The flight from New York is due to arrive soon. The changeover flight was held a little late in Minneapolis due to bad weather."

Manford nodded his head. "That's good for us," he said and forced his mind to go back to the streets and begin thinking like a street person. "We have to be smart, Sarah. Henry isn't a dummy."

Sarah nodded her head just as someone from airport security came on the line. "Yes, this is Detective Sarah Garland...Spencer...up in Snow Falls, Alaska. Who am I speaking to?"

"This is TSA Agent Lenny Miles," an annoyed voice replied. The voice belonged to a twenty-year-old guy who was thinner than a broomstick and weary like he hadn't slept in days. The unrelenting storms had made his recent shifts at the airport a long hardship. "What can I do for you, Detective?" Lenny asked, sitting in a small back office waiting for his coffee to reheat in a tiny, filthy microwave. "I'm on my break, so make it fast."

"I need to speak to the supervising security officer, please," Sarah said, realizing Lenny was going to be less than helpful.

"Brad? He's out sick," Lenny informed Sarah. "Bunch of people are out sick. I've been working overtime for four days straight and I'm getting mighty sick of it, too."

Sarah closed her eyes. "Can I speak to the person in charge?"

"That's me," Lenny told Sarah. "Like I said, lots of people are out sick. We're working skeleton crews. Besides that, the entire airport is a mess. Those hackers who got into the state database also scrambled the computers here at the airport. They managed to get the computers back up, but it's a mess. Lines are backed up, people are stranded all over the airport, but at least the flights are starting to get back on track."

"I didn't hear that it affected the airport."

"No one has," Lenny told Sarah, "so keep it under your hat, okay?"

Sarah shook her head. People like Lenny Miles gave those in positions of authority a bad name. "Listen, Leonard—"

"Look," Lenny said, interrupting Sarah, "if this is about looking for a missing person, just file a report and send it over, okay? We'll post it up for the guys to watch whoever comes through. I'm up to my ears with complaining passengers who are mad because they had to wait a few extra hours to board a stupid jet. I don't have time to brown-nose a cop about whatever runaway kid you're after, okay?"

Sarah felt like snapping at Lenny but knew she would be wasting her breath. "A flight is arriving from New York. A passenger named Henry Billinger is on the flight. When the flight arrives, could you please hold Henry Billinger in the airport security holding room?"

"Why?" Lenny asked.

"Because the man is a threat, that's why," Sarah said, losing her temper. The last thing she felt like doing was dealing with a snot-nosed brat who thought he was in charge of the entire Anchorage airport.

Lenny sipped his lukewarm coffee and made a face. "I'll keep a lookout," he lied. Lenny wasn't about to be tied up with paperwork all night. When his shift ended, his backside was leaving the airport as fast as possible. He had a bed waiting for him—a bed he hadn't seen in almost three days.

"I would appreciate that," Sarah told Lenny.

"Sure, yeah," Lenny said. "Is that all, Detective?"

"For now."

"Good," Lenny said and dumped the phone in his hand down.

Sarah rolled her eyes. "Little prick," she mumbled, hung up the phone, and turned to Amanda, Manford and Amy. "Hackers got at the airport, too," she explained. "Also, it seems most of the airport security is out sick. You might have overheard...I don't think whoever they left in charge is exactly on top of their game, security-wise. So I don't think Henry Billinger is going to have a difficult time getting in."

Amanda tapped her chin. "So we'll all go to my cabin for the night and tomorrow we'll come back, hide in the woods, wait for Henry to show up, and arrest him."

Sarah nodded her head. "That's what I was thinking, June Bug," she agreed. "You're turning out to be one smart cookie."

Amanda blushed. "Well...experience matters."

"I agree with what you two are saying, except for the part about leaving. This is my home now," Manford said. "If I run away tonight and lose my chance to get Billinger, I'll...well, I'll never forgive myself. I have to stay right here," Manford told Sarah and Amanda. "I swear on my mother's heart...I can't leave."

"What do you think?" Amanda asked Sarah.

"I don't think Billinger can make Snow Falls before morning," Sarah explained. "Roads this far north are icy and dangerous to drive on at night. Driving will be slow going." Sarah walked over to the kitchen table, picked up her coffee, took a sip, and then focused on the back door. "Snow is predicted for tomorrow," she continued. "Maybe the snow will work to our advantage."

"So we're staying put, love?" Amanda asked.

"I think we're safe for tonight," Sarah nodded her head, even though she felt spending the night at Amanda's cabin would be much safer. However, she knew that if Manford was forced to run, the fight stirring in his heart would be ripped out of him. Besides, she reminded herself, Macy Appleson was dead, and the killer was still on the loose. Conrad might object to everyone relocating to Amanda's cabin in the dark. "I better drive Amy home."

"We'll all drive Amy home," Amanda told Sarah.

Amy sighed. "I guess our night has come to an end," she told Manford. "I'm sorry it turned out this way."

"Maybe we can have dinner again?" Manford asked. "I mean, when all the trouble is over."

"I would love that," Amy beamed. She reached across the table and touched Manford's hand. "You're really sweet, Manford. I...like you."

"I don't know why," Manford confessed, staring at Amy's soft hand. "I invite you to dinner and instead get you involved in a takedown of a violent man from my past..." He began to put himself down and then stopped when he looked up into Amy's pretty eyes. "I like you too, Amy," he smiled. "I think...you're beautiful."

Amy blushed. "No one has ever called me beautiful before. The guys back in Maryland and New York treated me like I was a little kid, or a juvenile delinquent. My brother always told me I was a face on a billboard—pretty, but untouchable."

"You're more than a face on a billboard to me," Manford promised. He held Amy's hand tentatively. "I don't know how things are going to go with Henry, but if I survive the lion's attack, I sure would like to see you again...as friends, first. Conrad told me being friends is more important than...romance."

"Maybe romance can come later. It sure does seem to be in the air," Amy blushed again. "But yeah, being friends first sure would be great."

Amanda smiled at Sarah. "The little stud," she whispered.

"Indeed," Sarah agreed, feeling very proud of him. "Well, we better get you home, Amy."

Amy smiled at Manford, stood up, and walked to the back door. "I guess spending the night with my mom watching reruns of the Andy Griffith Show won't be too bad."

Manford hurried to help Amy put her coat on. His shorter arms barely reached up high enough to help, but he stood on his tiptoes to help her get settled. "All set?" he asked.

"All set," Amy smiled at Manford and then, to everyone's surprise, she bent down and gently kissed Manford. "That's for being a perfect gentleman."

Manford nearly melted down to the floor. His eyes became fuzzy and his voice goofy. "Uh...thanks..."

Amanda rolled her eyes. "Put your coat on, Romeo."

Sarah began to laugh but stopped when the telephone rang. "Maybe that's one of Conrad's friends calling from New York?" she said and answered the call. "Hello?"

"Hello, Detective Spencer," Henry hissed. "How nice to hear your voice again."

Sarah drew in a deep breath. "You're going to be arrested as soon as you step off the plane," she promised Henry, knowing her threat held no truth. She needed to keep Henry shaken up but didn't have a whole lot of tools to work with. Alaska wasn't Los Angeles or New York.

"It's him," Manford whispered to Amy and took her hand.

"Oh, I'm not flying into Anchorage," Henry laughed, sitting behind the wheel of a rental car. "I changed my mind and decided to go back to New York," he lied. "You can tell Manford that there are no hard feelings between us, okay? And no hard feelings between you and me. I know I lost my temper earlier, and I'm very sorry for that. I do hope you can forgive me." The slime in his voice practically oozed down the telephone line.

"You're lying through your teeth," Sarah informed Henry.

Henry glared out a cold, icy highway. He narrowed his eyes. "Detective—"

"The Feds are waiting for you back in New York, Mr. Billinger. They want to know why you've been forcing illegal aliens to work in your circus?"

Henry threw his foot on the brake. The rental car skidded off the road, nearly landing in a ditch. "Did that little rat tell you that?" he yelled. "Lies!"

"You're not a very smart man," Sarah told Henry. "The Feds have been eying you for a while."

"You're lying!" Henry blasted. "I can outsmart every Fed there is. I would know if I was being watched."

"Does it really matter?" Sarah asked in disbelief. "You've already turned yourself into a criminal on the run. And that, Mr. Billinger, was a very stupid thing to do."

Henry struck the steering wheel with his left fist, feeling, for the first time in his life, very stupid indeed. For once, he wasn't in control. As a matter of fact, he had allowed his temper back at the airport in New York to get the best of him, which had caused him a whole world of trouble. He had hoped, after having time to calm down, that sweet-talking Sarah—instead of killing her—might ease over the bumps in the road, but now it was clear he was caught between two speeding trains and nowhere else to go. "So be it," he said, gritting his teeth, "this is one fight Henry Billinger isn't going to lose. I'm going to feed that little rat to my lions one way or the other. And you," he warned Sarah, "will be next. And you can take this phone call to every cop in the world and let them listen to my voice, do you hear me!"

Sarah wished the phone call was being recorded. All she had to go off of was her word against the word of a crook —a crook who was determined to kill Manford Sappers.

"I'm on my way, detective," Henry warned. "And trust me, the circus always has a few extra tricks that the crowd doesn't know about." Henry ended the call, stepped on the gas, and sped away into the dark, icy night, driving away from Juneau like a dark creature crawling out of a bottomless ocean, starving for its next prey.

CHAPTER SEVEN

Henry was filled with too much rage to care about what might be happening in New York. So what if the Feds closed down his circus? So what if they came after him for hiring a few illegal aliens to clean up animal poop? So what if the IRS audited him for squirrelling away a few pennies here and there? It wasn't like he would be losing an empire.

The circus Henry owned was nothing more than a dump that had been painted over with a few pretty pieces of glitter here and there. It wasn't like the performers he hired were the world's most talented circus acts, either. At best, Henry knew, driving down a snowy road—a road shaking off the night and becoming lit by an early morning light—the high wire and cannonball acts were the only real attractions the circus had to offer. Everything else was shabby: the clown act was pathetic, the animals were mangy and the food was horrible. Yet a sucker was indeed born every minute. People with absolutely no sense paid good money to sit in sticky seats under a smelly tent and watch his lousy show. They paid their tickets, and that was what Henry depended on. The money from those tickets was what that thief Manford Sappers had stolen, and he was determined to get it back.

"I can always start over under a new name. Henry Billinger ain't stupid." Henry began thinking of all the fake identities he had stored in a safety deposit box. "I've started over two times before," he said. "Henry Billinger will come out number one again. New acts. New paint and new wheels. All it takes is a bunch of suckers to buy tickets and I'll be rolling in dough again."

As Henry drove down the snowy road, he spotted a black truck up ahead. The truck was parked on the side of the road. As Henry neared the truck, he saw a man step out onto the road and begin waving his arms. Henry considered running the man down but then had a sudden idea. He grinned, slowed down to a crawl, and eased up to the man. "What seems to be the problem, neighbor?" he asked in a smooth voice.

A man in his mid-thirties glared at Henry with suspicious eyes. "My truck just died on me," he said.

Henry nodded his head. "Happens," he said, staring at the man. The man was dressed in a black leather jacket, black pants and black motorcycle boots. Henry, being a man who could read a person like an open book, clearly saw the stranger wasn't a native to Alaska. "Sure, it happens," he said, lifting his eyes up to the man's scarred face fringed with a mangy mullet haircut.

"I'm not much good with engines," the man lied. "Maybe you can take a look?"

Henry saw the man keeping his right hand in the front pocket of his jacket. He knew the man was holding a gun and preparing to rob him, take the car, maybe even kill him. "Uh...sure, stranger. Let me back up a little and pull my car behind your truck," he said and then flashed a dark grin. "You're in luck because I just so happen to be a mechanic," he prattled away, making easy conversation to distract the man.

The man nodded his head and stepped over to the driver's side door of the truck. Henry rolled up the car window, put his car in reverse, eased back a few feet, put the car in drive, and then slammed on the gas. The man preparing to kill Henry—the man who had killed Mrs. Appleson and her daughter—didn't stand a chance. Before he could run even two steps from the charging vehicle, Henry plowed him down.

"Well, now," Henry chuckled, "I just did the world a favor, now didn't I? I might have just killed a dangerous criminal." Henry stepped out of the car, looked around, saw only white woods, a low, dark gray sky, and air filled with wet snowflakes being tossed about by an icy wind.

No witnesses. "Perfect," he grinned, hurried over to the black truck, and began investigating the interior. To his relief, the keys to the truck were still in the ignition. "Let's see," Henry said, crawling into the driver's seat, and turned the key in the ignition. The truck roared to life. "Ah," Henry grinned. He checked the gas gauge, found the needle pointing to half full, and grinned again. "You did a no-no, didn't you?" he asked the dead man. "You needed to ditch this truck and get you a new vehicle. Oldest trick in the book. Takes one to know one, my friend."

Henry turned off the truck and continued to investigate the interior. He located a small black bag holding a second gun, a few thousand dollars in cash, and some fake identification papers. "My, who did I kill?" Henry pondered. "No matter, seems like luck is on my side."

Henry was unaware that he had run down the professional killer that Macy Appleson had hired to kill her mother. Henry was also unaware that the killer had turned on Macy, ended her life, and fled Snow Falls after Macy had refused to pay up the full promised amount, threatening to turn the hitman over to the cops instead. But what did Henry care? He had a gun, a new vehicle and some extra cash to work with—along with some fake identification papers. "If I had known Alaska was the land of easy money, I would have moved here a long time ago," he chuckled.

Henry climbed out of the truck, grabbed the arms of the dead body, pulled it as deep into the woods as he could manage in the drifts of snow, then drove his car off the road and hurried back to the truck. He grabbed a lug wrench out of the bed of the truck, ran back to his rental car, and broke out all of the windows and headlights. Satisfied, he threw the wrench into the woods, gathered his personal belongings from the car, hurried back to the truck, crawled into the driver's seat, and sped away.

"Now the cops will think that poor old Henry has become the victim of a horrible crime," he laughed. "Snow Falls, here I come."

As Henry sped away in a stolen truck, Manford walked into Sarah's kitchen half asleep. "I didn't sleep very well," he confessed, still wearing the same clothes from the night before. "Every time I dozed off, I dreamed of Henry."

"I'll fix you a cup of coffee," Sarah told Henry.

Manford pointed at Mittens. "I need to walk her first." Manford retrieved Mittens' leash. "Is Conrad home?" he asked, attaching the leash to Mittens. Mittens wagged her tail and licked Manford's hand.

"No," Sarah explained. "The system came back online late last night. He's at the station getting caught up on his work."

Manford carefully walked Mittens to the back door and

put on his coat. Poor Mittens still had a bad limp. "I hope he finds out something," he said.

"I'm sure Conrad is making his keyboard smoke as we speak," Sarah assured Manford, glanced at the kitchen clock, and bit down on her lip. "It's nearly nine o'clock," she said. "I want to get into town soon, okay? Amanda already left."

"Left?" Manford asked in a worried voice.

"Amanda's husband called her about two hours ago. He needed Amanda to go back to their cabin and locate a legal document he needed." Sarah took a sip of coffee. "Amanda wasn't too happy, but...love makes a person drive home even in freezing snow."

Manford stared at Sarah and locked his eyes on the gray wool dress she was wearing. "You look like you've been up for a while, too," he said and nodded down at the brown boots on Sarah's feet. It was clear that Sarah was dressed for action. "You're worried, aren't you?"

"Let's just say I think it's best if we stay in town today," Sarah explained. "Andrew already has two of his guys watching my cabin as we speak. If Henry shows up here, they'll nab him."

"Two cops are outside?" Manford asked, checking the window.

Sarah nodded his head. "Andy and Hank," she said.

"They are good men, honey. They know this land like the back of their hands." Sarah put down her coffee. "It's better if we let the cops handle Henry out here instead of trying to nab him ourselves," she explained, leaving out the part that Conrad had ordered Andy and Hank to watch the cabin while demanding his dear wife get her tush into town so he could watch over her personally. Conrad didn't like the fact that Henry had called his home after he had raced off to Mrs. Appleson's cabin—he didn't like the fact that Henry had threatened his wife for a second time and surely wasn't going to let his wife remain in danger.

Manford looked down at Mittens. "Well, I guess that does make sense. I mean, I was prepared to go stand out in the woods and stake out this place...Henry is sure to show up here." Manford drew in a deep, sleepy breath. "If you think it's better to let the cops stake out the cabin...okay, then."

Sara began to speak but stopped when the telephone rang. "That's Conrad," she said and nodded at the back door. "Hurry and walk Mittens." Manford agreed and walked Mittens out into a heavy falling snow. As soon as Manford was outside, Sarah grabbed the phone. "Conrad?"

"It's me," Conrad said, sitting behind his desk.

"What do you have, honey?" Sarah asked in an urgent voice.

"Mrs. Appleson has a one-million-dollar life insurance policy. Macy Appleson was the sole beneficiary, unsurprisingly," Conrad explained and fought back a yawn. He was used to long nights and cold weather, but this had been an especially long night.

Sarah rubbed her chin. "Macy hired someone to kill her mother...but got herself killed in the process," she said.

"That's what I'm thinking," Conrad nodded his head, grabbed a brown coffee mug, and gulped down some coffee. "Last month Macy drained her savings account. She took out twenty thousand dollars." Conrad set his coffee down. "My guess is that money included a down payment for a hitman."

"You did some checking?"

"I did," Conrad nodded his head. "I checked out the prisons in California," he explained. "I was coming up empty-handed, just guys released for drugs, robbery...nothing too serious. But then I came across a guy named Ridge Klopedale." Conrad put down his coffee. "Klopedale has a bad criminal history, Sarah. He's been convicted for assault more times than I can count. The guy was finally sent to prison for being hired out as a hitman...hired to kill some woman's ex-husband."

Sarah shook her head. "The world is a very ugly place."

"You're telling me," Conrad agreed. "And what makes this world an even uglier place is the prison system. Ridge

Klopedale didn't even serve half of his prison sentence. He was released early for good behavior." Conrad shook his head. "Sarah, this guy served barely a quarter of his time...it's enough to make you sick."

"It sure is."

Conrad fought back another yawn. "Anyway, honey, I checked out who visited Ridge Klopedale while he was in prison and—"

"And Macy Appleson was on the visitor's log, right?"

"Macy marked herself as his girlfriend. Guess the woman was into bad guys. Or was willing to pretend, anyway, in order to hire one."

"And found out the hard way that walking dark alleys leads to death," Sarah pointed out.

"Yeah," Conrad said, rubbed the back of his neck, and then shook his head. "I have a statewide APB out on Ridge Klopedale. He owns a black Dodge truck, so the state police are pulling over any and all black trucks. The airport is on alert and the border crossing folks have been notified. If Ridge Klopedale is still in Alaska, the only way he's getting out is on foot."

"Chances are he's still in Alaska," Sarah told Conrad.

"Maybe," Conrad said and then moved off into another room in his tired mind. "Now, we need to talk about Henry Billinger."

"What do you have?"

"Billinger grabbed a rental car in Juneau," Conrad explained. "He changed flights in Minneapolis and flew into Juneau instead of Anchorage."

Sarah closed her eyes. "Please tell me you have an APB out on his rental car?"

"Honey, you know me better than that."

Sarah sighed. "Of course, I do...I'm sorry."

"I know you're worried about Manford," Conrad told Sarah. "I know better than to be offended."

Sarah opened her eyes. "So Henry is on his way to Snow Falls."

"Yeah...I think we can assume that now," Conrad agreed in a miserable voice. "And my guess is—"

"He isn't going to just waltz into town in a rental car," Sarah finished for Conrad. "That sleazebag is going to try and trick us, Conrad. He's going to sneak into town under the radar...somehow."

Conrad stared at his coffee mug. "Long drive from Juneau to Snow Falls," he pointed out. "The best we can do is watch our own roads and keep watch on the cabin."

"And wait..." Sarah felt anger grip her heart. "I hate it when the bad guys have the upper hand," she told

Conrad and stomped the floor. "I don't like being in the dark."

"That's the way the bad guys play...most of them, anyway," Conrad told Sarah. He leaned back in his office chair. "Honey, you and Manford drive into town as soon as possible, okay? I want you guys to spend the day with me at the station."

"Not the station...uh, how about O'Mally's and then...my coffee shop?" Sarah asked. "If I take Manford to the station, it might spook him all over again. He'll think we're giving Henry Billinger too much credit."

"We don't know what Billinger is capable of—"

"I know, honey...but we don't need to let Manford know how worried we are," Sarah said.

"But we are. We are worried for good reason."

Sarah closed her eyes, saw Manford's determined face in her mind, and sighed. "I know we are," she said and nodded her head, feeling like a parent pacing the floors over a child that was out past their curfew. She saw a fat blob of a man reach out from a thick darkness, grab Manford, and throw him into the mouth of a hungry lion. "I'll stay in public places...and Amanda will be with me...we'll hang out at O'Mally's, let Manford see Amy...go to my coffee shop...have lunch at the diner...and near evening time I'll bring Manford to the station, okay?"

Conrad didn't want to agree with Sarah, but he was tired, in need of a nap, and figured as long as Sarah stayed in public places, she would be okay. At least until evening. "Okay," he caved in. "But call me every hour."

"I will," Sarah promised.

Conrad rubbed the back of his tired neck. "I'm going to grab a quick nap in one of the cells, honey. Andrew is in his office. Call him when you get to O'Mally's. In the meantime, I'll keep Andy and Hank out at the cabin."

Sarah heard Manford walk up to the back door. "Every hour," she promised.

"I'll see you around five," Conrad said. "We'll have something to eat at the diner and then make a plan from there, okay?"

"I love you."

"Love you, too."

Sarah hung up the phone as Manford opened the kitchen door. She watched him walk inside with Mittens, stomp snow off his boots, and look at her with worried eyes. "What do you say we grab a muffin, pick Amanda up, and go to O'Mally's and spend some time with Amy?"

Manford read Sarah's eyes. She tried to look cheerful, but he knew something was horribly wrong.

Sarah watched Amanda wander off into the heart of O'Mally's with an empty shopping cart. Only Amanda could find the presence of mind to shop in the middle of a crisis. "She's something," Sarah sighed and turned her attention back to Manford. Manford was standing at the snack counter talking to Amy. Amy sure seemed to like Manford, which pleased Sarah's heart. "They do make a sweet couple," she said, walked over to a booth, sat down, and picked up a cup of hot chocolate. "Sometimes a woman just needs chocolate," Sarah whispered but stopped when the cell phone in her purse buzzed. She calmly put down the hot chocolate, stood up and waved at Manford. "I'm going to the ladies' room," she called out.

"Oh...okay," Manford said in an uneasy voice. He didn't want Sarah leaving his eyesight. Not because he was afraid—well, he was afraid—but because he didn't want any harm to come to Sarah. "Try to, you know, hurry."

"I will," Sarah promised and walked away toward the back of the store where the bathrooms were located. She spotted Amanda standing in front of a rack of sweaters, shook her head, and walked up to her. "Any luck?"

Amanda made a sad face. "I'm wearing a one-of-a-kind dress that needs the perfect cardigan to go with it...but does old man O'Mally order cardigans in the right color? No."

Sarah looked at the light peach dress Amanda was

171

wearing. The dress was very lovely, appeared warm, and was very modest. She had to admit, a lovely cardigan would have complimented the dress. "Keep searching."

"I will," Amanda promised in a determined voice.

Sarah smiled, took out her cell phone, and returned Conrad's call. "It's me, honey."

"Bad news," Conrad said, fighting to keep his eyes open. "Billinger's rental car was found on Old Route 19."

"Old Route 19?" Sarah asked.

"A rarely used route that the truckers mostly use," Conrad explained. "The route runs somewhere between Fairbanks and Anchorage, at least that's what the state police told me. I'm not familiar with every road in the state, so I'm taking their word for it."

Sarah watched Amanda mumble something to herself. "Did the state police find a body?"

"A trucker spotted the rental car," Conrad explained, "and called the state police." Conrad gulped down more coffee. "Honey, Billinger wasn't found."

"But...?" Sarah asked, reading Conrad's voice.

"The rental car was pretty broken up." Conrad rubbed his eyes. "A K-9 unit was called in, Sarah, and the dog managed to locate a body."

"But not...Henry Billinger?" Sarah said, feeling her stomach tighten.

"No. It was Ridge Klopedale," Conrad announced in an upset voice. "The state police told me the guy looked like he had been plowed down." Conrad shook his head. "I don't know...my guess is...somehow...I don't know...Billinger met up with Klopedale? It seems like an awful coincidence. It makes no sense. I don't know how Billinger knew him. Honey, I don't really have a theory at this moment."

Sarah heard frustration consume her husband's voice. "We'll figure this out, honey. I promise."

Conrad rubbed his nose again. "The state police told me the windows on the rental were smashed in with a lug wrench they found in the woods. My guess is Billinger tried to make it seem like he was in some kind of an accident to throw the police off track."

"The police found Klopedale's body and a broken up rental car," Sarah nodded her head. "Seems to me that Billinger is hoping the police will see him as a victim and not the aggressor." Sarah grew silent for a second. "Or," she said, feeling a new thought enter her mind, "maybe he attempted to fake his own death?"

"I'm all ears," Conrad said, leaned forward in his office chair, and waited.

Sarah bit down on her lip and walked over to a wooden

rack holding winter dresses. "Conrad...Billinger knows he's in trouble, right?"

"I would assume."

"So what if...what if he killed Klopedale and smashed up the rental car to make it appear like...he had been kidnapped, or even killed himself?"

"Right now, the state police have no other choice but to believe Billinger's life is in danger," Conrad said in a regretful voice. "The snow in that area is pretty heavy, and every tire track has been covered over. They don't have much to go on."

"And that's what Billinger wants." Sarah pushed a dark green dress to the side and studied a lighter colored green dress with white stripes. For a second, she imagined herself standing in the warm department store, surrounded by dresses, smelling the cozy scent of peppermint and simply shopping without a worry in the world. "Honey, did the state police find any other vehicle at the scene?"

"No," Conrad replied. "If Klopedale was driving a black truck, the truck is now missing."

"Maybe Billinger took it?"

"Maybe," Conrad agreed. "All I know is that there's a storm moving our way."

"I know. I checked the weather," Sarah told Conrad.

"The storm that's traveling toward us is going to be a rough one."

"This entire winter has been rough, and it's far from being over."

Sarah bit down on her lip. "Any suggestions?"

"Stay in town," Conrad told Sarah in a firm voice. "We'll stay at the station and keep the cabin under surveillance. Billinger is bound to show up sooner or later and when he does, we'll snatch him."

"How about if we stay at Amanda's cabin?" Sarah asked. "I really don't want Manford to feel like we're backing down, Conrad. At least if we stay at Amanda's, he'll feel better. Besides, Billinger doesn't know where Amanda lives."

Conrad considered Sarah's suggestion. "Okay," he said. "I'll meet you at Amanda's cabin in a few hours. Right now, I have some more work to do."

"You need a nap first."

"No time," Conrad said. "I tried to take a quick nap earlier, but my phone kept me awake."

"Oh, honey."

"The life of a cop," Conrad told Sarah. He finished off his coffee. "I'll meet you at Amanda's around five."

"I'll get us dinner from the diner, okay?"

"Sounds good," Conrad yawned. "Sarah?"

"Yes, honey?"

"How in the world are Billinger and Klopedale linked?" he asked in a worried voice.

"You mean...you think maybe...Manford is hiding something? Like he knows Macy somehow?"

"That's the only explanation my mind can grab onto. I mean, honey, did Manford really show up in Snow Falls by accident?"

Sarah sighed. "I don't know," she confessed.

Conrad saw Andrew stick his head into his office. "A black truck was found deserted outside of Fairbanks."

"Honey, I have to go. I'll call you in a bit."

"Okay." Sarah ended the call and walked back to Amanda. "Bad news," she said and explained to her best friend the news Conrad had tossed into her lap.

Amanda frowned. "What now?"

"Can we stay at your cabin?"

"You better believe your toasty muffins you can...and you are," Amanda told Sarah. She grabbed Sarah's arm. "You're not leaving my eyesight from this point forward."

"It's not my life that I'm worried about," Sarah told Amanda. "I'm worried sick about Manford."

"You think short stuff is hiding something?" Amanda asked.

"Well...yes and no," Sarah admitted in a miserable voice. "Klopedale is dead. Billinger is missing and his rental car was located where Klopedale's body was found." Sarah looked toward the snack bar. "Come on, June Bug, I have to talk with Manford."

Amanda grabbed the shopping cart and walked back to the snack bar with Sarah. "I'll keep Amy company. You talk with Manford."

"Okay," Sarah said. She waved at Manford. "Uh...can we talk?" she asked.

Manford didn't like the expression on Sarah's face. He looked at Amy with worried eyes and slowly walked over to the booth where Sarah was standing. "What's wrong?"

Sarah sat down. "Conrad called me," she said and motioned for Manford to sit down. Manford drew in a worried breath and sat down across from Sarah. "You see," she said, struggling for a calm way to approach Manford without upsetting him, "A man name Ridge Klopedale was found dead."

"Who?" He looked wholly confused.

"A man who was hired by Macy Appleson to murder her mother...or so it appears." Sarah stared into Manford's worried eyes. How in the world was she going to tell him the truth without making it seem like she was also throwing guilt into the air? "The rental car Henry Billinger was driving was found where Ridge Klopedale's body was found."

Manford could only look at Sarah with confused eyes. "I don't...understand."

"Neither do we," Sarah confessed. "Do you have any idea how Henry Billinger could be connected to a man hired to kill a woman with a...one-million-dollar life insurance policy?"

"One million..." Manford's eyes grew wide. And then a horrible truth clicked in his worried mind—a truth that attacked the fog hanging over his eyes. "Hey...you think I'm involved in the Appleson murders somehow?"

"No...honey, no. Conrad and I just aren't sure how Billinger and Klopedale are connected. And...well, you did show up right when Mrs. Appleson was killed. And then it seems Billinger went right to where Klopedale was waiting. It could all be a coincidence, but the timing...to any cop...would seem suspicious."

Manford stared into Sarah's eyes. "I...told you everything. I trusted you," he said in an upset voice. "I thought you trusted me. And now you're...betraying me? You're...just like everyone else." Manford shot to his feet.

Amy saw Manford stand up and begin shaking his head

at Sarah. "Something's the matter," she told Amanda and ran over to Manford. "What's going on?" she asked.

"What's going on?" Manford repeated in a bitter tone. He threw his hand at Sarah. "I'm being accused of two murders, that's what's the matter."

"No, I'm not—"

"Yes, you are!" Manford yelled. "You think I'm...no good. You think I'm involved with some killing...for money..." Manford looked up at Amanda with hurt eyes, then he looked at Amy. His heart broke into a million pieces and then filled with fury. "You're all the same...all of you!" he yelled and began backing away from the booth.

"Manford...please..." Amy began to plead.

"All the same...just like my old man. The only person I could ever trust was my mother...and she's dead!" Tears began to flow out of Manford's eyes. "You're all the same...you think I'm trash, a thief, a murderer? You're all fake. All of you!" Manford turned and ran out of O'Mally's.

"Manford!" Amy yelled, stricken.

Amanda gently grabbed Amy's arm. "Let Sarah go after him, love."

Sarah felt a tear release from her eye. "I guess I better," she said and slowly stood up. "I'm not sure what I'm going to say when I find him, though. He...seems to hate me."

"He's upset," Amanda told Sarah. "I can't tell you how many times my son told me he wished I had turned into a different mother while he was growing up, love." Amanda patted Sarah's shoulder. "The anger will pass after he calms down and learns the truth. You're just trying to figure out a tangled web; he's got a lot of old pain and fear weighing him down. He doesn't know you have his best interests at heart."

Sarah looked into Amanda's loving, wise eyes. Amanda had raised a son. She was a mother. If anyone knew how Manford was feeling right now, it would be her. "What do I say to him, June Bug?" she begged.

"Just offer him love," Amanda whispered and wiped Sarah's tear away.

Sarah drew in a deep breath, looked at Amy, and hurried outside into a heavy falling snow. Manford was nowhere in sight. "Manford?" she yelled and began following a set of boot prints in the snow. The prints led around to the side of O'Mally's, continued around to the back, and then, to Sarah's horror, ran straight into the woods. "Manford!" she cried out and dashed to the tree line. "Manford!"

Determined to find him, Sarah locked her eyes on the snow and began following the tracks. She walked no more than fifty yards and then stopped. "The tracks...where did they go?" she asked in a frantic voice, breathing white puffs of smoke from her mouth. "They just...vanished into thin air."

As Sarah searched for Manford's footsteps, Manford continued to climb up a high tree. When he reached a steady limb, he threw his eyes down, spotted Sarah desperately searching for him, and shook his head. "It's for the best," he whispered and fought back tears. "Guess this old circus trick paid off...now if she'll just go away...go away..."

"Manford!" Sarah called out in a hurt voice, casting her gaze around her in the snowy woods frantically, still seeing nothing. "Please...honey...come back so we can talk! I wasn't accusing you of anything. I was only hoping you could help me understand what's going on...three people are dead...I'm worried sick about you...please!"

Manford wanted to believe Sarah but he just couldn't. "Liar," he whispered and felt a tear drop from his eye. But he stayed quiet, willing her not to see him. "They're all liars...I should have known better...I should have kept my street clothes." Manford wiped his tear away as an icy gust of wind struck his body. "Never trust anybody...rules of the street...never trust anybody."

Sarah threw her eyes in every possible direction. Fear and panic raced through her heart. "Manford...honey...please! Billinger is on his way to Snow Falls! It's not safe alone! Come back! Can you hear me? Where are you?"

"I'll...handle Billinger," Manford whispered in a shaky voice. "When Billinger arrives...he's gonna die...or I'll die trying to kill him." Manford grew silent, watched Sarah continue her frantic search, and then closed his eyes. "Just go away...go away...you're all the same."

Sarah wasn't prepared to give up. She whipped out her cell phone and began to call Conrad. "No," she said desperately, reading *No Service* on the screen. "I'm out too far. I have to go back to the store." Sarah threw her eyes around the deep, snowy white woods again, bit down on her lip, and then dashed away.

"That's right...run away," Manford whispered as tears began to flood from his eyes. "I knew you would. You're all the same...all the same."

Sarah, with tears falling from her own eyes, ran back to the front of O'Mally's where her cell phone finally picked up a signal. She called Conrad. "Conrad, Manford ran off."

"What do you mean he ran off?" Conrad asked. He jumped up from behind his desk and waved his hand at Andrew.

"I...asked him about Billinger and Klopedale...I asked him about Mrs. Appleson's insurance policy," Sarah cried. "Manford accused me of saying he was involved...then he ran off. I followed his tracks into the woods, but they vanished into thin air. Please, get every available man down here. We have to find Manford. It's not safe in this storm. We have to find him."

"Yes, we do," Conrad said in a worried voice. "A black truck was found outside of Fairbanks. The truck was reported stolen last week." Conrad grabbed his leather jacket. "I'm not sure what Billinger is up to, but he's getting closer."

"Hurry," Sarah begged as the heavy snow coated her trembling body. "Manford is in danger."

Far away, Henry Billinger grinned as he drove toward Snow Falls in a run-down pickup truck he had bought from an old man for an even two thousand dollars cash. "You never know what you're going to find in Alaska," he laughed and added a little more speed to the truck.

CHAPTER EIGHT

H enry drove the truck he had bought down a snowy driveway, forcing the tires through deep snow, parked in front of an empty cabin lathered in snow and nodded his head.

"Manford...I'm here," he hissed.

Without wasting another second, he climbed out of the truck and stepped into a strong storm. "What a perfect day to die," he laughed and quickly eyed the cabin. It was clear that the cabin was empty. Henry had no desire to force his way into the cabin, though. He was a man on a mission. "Time for a little fire," he whispered, quickly grabbed a metal gas can from the bed of his truck and made his way to the cabin through knee-deep snow. "Time for a grand bonfire," he whispered again as the icy wind and snow tore into his distorted face, grabbing at the cheap black coat and gloves he had purchased hastily in Minneapolis.

After dousing the entire outside of the cabin with gas, Henry quickly climbed up onto a snow-covered porch, broke a front window out with the metal gas can, threw gas into a front living room and then backed away. "Thar she blows," he whispered, threw down the metal gas can, snatched a cigarette lighter from the front pocket of his coat and lit the gas. The gas erupted into a bright, fiery trail, rushing through the snow toward the cabin, and then exploded in a bright flash of fire. "Perfect," Henry laughed, warming his hands against the flames for a moment before he ran back to his truck, and set out to burn a few more empty cabins.

By noontime, over seven rental cabins were sending noxious dark gray smoke up into the icy winter sky.

"That's cabin number seven," Andrew told Conrad in a furious voice. He slammed down his phone, grabbed a gray winter hat, tossed it on his head and shook his head. "Our boys can't keep up with the fires. Good thing it's snowing. The snow won't let the fires spread far, but still..." Andrew shook his head again.

Conrad checked his gun. "Billinger is in town," he said and threw his eyes at Sarah. Sarah and Amanda were standing in the doorway of Andrew's office. "Nothing?" he asked.

"No," Sarah said in an upset voice. "It's been nearly twenty-four hours since Manford ran off."

Conrad didn't know what to say. Both Sarah and Amanda were tired, still wearing the same clothes they had been wearing when Manford vanished, but both still held the desire to fight in their eyes. But fight what? A bunch of fires? "You girls stay here at the station. I'm going to ride out to the fires and start looking around."

Sarah began to object when the phone on Andrew's desk rang. "Not another fire," Andrew begged and answered the call. "Yeah, this is Chief—"

"I want to speak to Detective Sarah Spencer," Henry hissed. "If I don't, more cabins will burn...only, next time I won't skip the cabins that have people inside."

Andrew looked at Sarah. "It's Billinger...he wants to talk to you."

Sarah rushed to Andrew's desk and took the phone. "What do you want?" she snapped in fury.

"I want Manford," Henry growled. "If Manford isn't delivered to me within the next hour, I'm going to begin burning down the cabins that aren't empty. Do I make myself perfectly clear?" Henry hissed.

"Manford ran away," Sarah told Henry. "I don't know where he is. But what I do know is that you're going to spend the rest of your miserable life in prison."

Henry gritted his teeth. "Don't try to threaten me," he snapped at Sarah.

"It's not a threat, it's a promise. Show your face, you coward, and I'll arrest you."

Henry felt his cheeks turn red. "Will you?" he asked in a poison voice as he slowly drove past the station house. With the storm raging and his truck blending in with every other run-down truck in Snow Falls, it was impossible for them to know who was driving down the front street. "Maybe I'll begin with you first, then?" he asked.

"Okay," Sarah agreed. "Begin with me, Billinger." Sarah looked at Conrad. "Where do you want to meet?"

"I'm not stupid, Detective," Henry informed Sarah. "I know how cops work." Henry drove past Sarah's coffee shop and came to a stop at the end of the street. "I'll meet —" before Henry could say another word, the driver's door to the truck exploded open. Henry threw his eyes to the side in shock and saw Manford appear holding a gun in his hand. Henry dropped the cell phone he was holding and quickly stepped on the gas. Manford, not willing to let Henry escape, dived into the cab of the truck and aimed his gun at the man's face.

"Do what I tell you...or die," Manford screamed in a shaky voice as the speeding truck skidded along in the snow. "I'll pull the trigger, Henry...I swear it."

Henry glanced down at Manford and saw that he was speaking the truth. Rage filled his mind. How in the world had this little person gotten the best of him? How had he foiled his perfect plan? "Where?" he asked, aiming the truck toward a residential neighborhood.

"Take a left. Onto Snow Mountain Drive. Number 177," Manford ordered Henry without realizing that Sarah was listening to his every word. "It's time to end this, Henry...once and for all. I'm not going to let you hurt Sarah...do you understand me?"

Sarah felt tears begin falling from her eyes. "Oh Manford," she whispered, listening in from the police station. The cell phone remained in Henry's hand, his conversation with Sarah forgotten.

Henry swallowed. He knew that Manford would make him eat a bullet if he dared make one wrong move. "You stupid idiot!" he yelled. "Do you really believe some cop cares about you?"

Manford scooted all the way in and finally slammed the door behind him, his back against the passenger door, putting as much distance between himself and Henry as possible. "Yesterday I wasn't so sure," he said as Henry maneuvered the truck through a snow-covered neighborhood lined with cozy cabins and cottages. "Yesterday I thought Sarah...Amanda...Conrad...they were all the same. But last night I had a lot of time to think, Henry. That's when I realized you were up to something...one of your devious plans. So I came to town, hid out in Sarah's coffee shop, waited until morning, and began watching the cop station. Sarah and Amanda showed up about an hour later...I figured it wouldn't be too long before you showed up."

Henry glared at Manford with eyes filled with fiery hatred. "How did you know I would show up in town?"

"Because you got too much pride," Manford explained, keeping the gun he had found in Sarah's coffee shop aimed right at Henry. "You can't resist circling your prey...just like you did my old man...my mom...and me."

Henry gritted his teeth. He wanted more than anything to lean over and strangle Manford but knew that if his hands even moved an inch in the little man's direction, he would be met with a bullet. So he shut his mouth and drove to 177 Snow Mountain Drive, as directed. As he drove through the storm, Henry forced his mind to think. There had to be a way. Sure, there had to be a way to win the fight, he thought as Manford directed him to the cabin.

"There," Manford said and pointed toward Sarah's cabin. He drew in a scared breath and tried to settle his nerves. According to the police scanner on the desk in Sarah's office back at the coffee shop, every cop in town had been called away to the fires, including Andy and Hank. Sarah's cabin was no longer being watched.

Henry eased the truck into an empty driveway and parked in front of Sarah's cabin. "What's your plan now?" he growled.

Manford reached into the front pocket of his coat with his left hand, pulled out a pair of handcuffs he had found in the coffee shop office, and threw them at Henry. "Put those on," he demanded.

Henry felt the handcuffs strike his fat belly. Then he looked into Manford's eyes. Manford had thought of everything and was still prepared to kill him on the spot. "Okay, Manford...I'll do it your way...for now," he growled, then slapped the handcuffs onto his wrists and gritted his teeth. "There."

"Get out of the truck, Henry," Manford ordered. He was scared to death but determined to have the faith of David. "I have to protect my friends," he told Henry. "I'm going to leave them a present...you. And then I'm going to vanish into the wind." Manford felt his heart break. "They've been real nice to me and I ain't caused them nothing but trouble. You're going to be my way of...saying thank you...now get out of the truck."

Henry growled and used one handcuffed hand to open the driver's side door, not realizing that his cell phone was still on and that Sarah was still listening. Manford quickly jumped out of the truck, trudged around the front of the truck, and pointed his gun at Henry. "Into the bed of the truck," he ordered, yelling over the icy winds.

When silence fell in the cab of the truck, Sarah slammed down the phone in her hand. "We have to hurry. Manford took Billinger to our cabin," she told Conrad.

"Get our guys out to the cabin," Conrad ordered Andrew and stormed away with Sarah and Amanda. He ran outside, dived into his truck, brought it to life, and sped away just as Amanda and Sarah managed to climb into the cab next to him.

"Into the bed!" Manford yelled at Henry.

Henry hissed at Manford. "What are you going to do? Make me sit in the snow?"

Manford drew a deep breath, aimed the gun at the ground, and fired off a warning shot. The gun's recoil nearly caused him to jump out of his skin. The gun shot scared Henry even worse. Henry Billinger, as deadly as he was, was terrified of guns. "Get in the bed of the truck...or else..."

"Okay, Manford...just calm down," Henry said, held his handcuffed wrists up into the snow, and nodded at the bed of the truck. "Just don't do anything stupid."

Manford was about ready to pass out with fear. Was he really getting the best of Henry Billinger? Was he really standing up to a bully...a killer? Was he really making his mother proud and proving his old man wrong, finally, after all these years? "Get into the back."

Henry nodded his head and struggled into the bed of the truck, sitting down next to a metal gas can. "Okay...I'm in," he said.

"Sit down!" Manford yelled. Henry dropped down, pressed himself up against the wall of the truck bed, and held up his hands. Manford quickly climbed up into the bed next to him. The time had come to kill Henry Billinger. But first he had work to do. "Okay," he said and pulled a tape recorder from his coat pocket, "it's time to confess."

Henry stared at the little black tape recorder—one that Manford had found stashed away in Sarah's desk in her office back at the coffee shop—and then looked up at Manford. "Confess what?"

"Everything! Mrs. Appleson...the man who killed her..." Manford snapped on the tape recorder. "I want you to confess that I had nothing to do with it, do you hear me? I want you to...tell Sarah that I'm innocent."

"Who is this Mrs. Appleson?" Henry asked in a confused, sneering voice. "Manford, you're not making any sense. Has the snow driven you insane as well as stupid?"

"Stop lying!" Manford yelled. His hands began to shake. "The man who killed Mrs. Appleson...the hitman...you killed him, didn't you? You found him somehow and Sarah thinks I'm connected..."

Henry stared at Manford and then leaned back his fat head and began laughing in surprise. "Oh, this is too good!"

"Stop laughing!" Manford warned Henry.

Henry leaned his head forward. "You stupid runt," he hissed. "I killed a...a backwoods hitman? Is that it? I didn't even know the man. I just happened to come across him on the road. The man tried to steal my car!" Henry roared. "I knew I just couldn't drive into Snow Falls, you stupid rat! I needed a plan, and that idiot man played perfectly into my hands!"

"You're...you're lying! Mrs. Appleson and her daughter are dead...she had a one-million-dollar life insurance policy. It must be something to do with you—"

Henry gritted his teeth. "You pathetic wart," he growled, "I'm telling you the truth. I don't even know the name of the man I ran down!" Henry narrowed his eyes. "I'm a man who thinks on his feet, Manford. You know that. I use whatever situation I can to help me and make it work out to my advantage. I live in the moment!"

"You—"

"I don't know the man I ran down or the two women you claimed he killed, you stupid idiot!" Henry roared.

Manford stared at Henry. To his dismay, he could clearly see the monster was actually speaking the truth. "But...then..." he stopped talking as confusion grabbed his mind. Could it be that mere coincidence was at play? Every mystery had a logical beginning...surely, Manford thought, coincidence couldn't be a player in this. No matter, he thought, struggling to push his confusion away; he had Henry, and that's what mattered. "Okay," he said, turned off the tape recorder, shoved it away, and aimed his gun at Henry, "you have no confession for me, that's fine. It's time to die."

Henry felt a strange, deep fear begin squeezing his heart. Manford was going to kill him...this little man that he had tortured for years was finally going to avenge his mother and himself. Justice had finally come back to find Henry and he had no place to run. And for the first time in his miserable existence...Henry Billinger was...terrified.

"Manford...we can talk..." he began to beg, feeling his temper freeze up like a block of ice, break off into the snow, and vanish into a dark pit. "You can keep the money you stole..."

Manford placed his left hand over his right hand and steadied his gun as icy winds and heavy snow struck his freezing face. "My mother has that money now...even in death you couldn't triumph over her. It belongs to her," he told Henry. "It always did, and it always will." Manford narrowed his eyes. "What I'm going to do today is no longer for my mother as much as it is for a different woman—a good, kind woman with a heart so true you would never understand it. You—you twisted fiend. This is for Sarah..."

Henry held up his manacled wrists. "No...Manford...please..." he begged, feeling death seeping from the snow. "I—"

"Shut your mouth," Manford ordered Henry as tears began rushing from his eyes. "You tortured my mother for years...you killed my old man...you tortured me, too...your time has come to die..." Manford raised his eyes and studied a deep, cold gray sky. "Finally," he whispered. "Mom...I'm finally going to do what I promised you. I'm going to get free."

Henry knew his time to die had arrived. If he didn't act, he was surely going to be killed. So he did all that his mind could think to do. He lifted both of his legs and with a mighty, strangled scream, lashed out and tried to kick Manford over the back tailgate. A shot rang out, and a scream pierced the air.

Sarah thought she heard a gunshot go off as Conrad swung onto her street at a high and dangerous speed. Conrad's truck nearly lost control and fishtailed around the corner, narrowly avoiding the ditch and the heavy drifts of snow. Conrad managed to get control of the truck at the last second. "Hold on!" he yelled and floored it toward Sarah's cabin.

"I'm holding...I'm holding, you insane man!" Amanda screamed, holding onto the passenger door handle for dear life.

Conrad zoomed down the street and slammed to a stop when he saw a strange truck parked in the cabin's driveway. "There's Manford!" he yelled. He jumped out of the truck.

Sarah and Amanda spilled out of the truck and spotted Manford aiming a gun at a large, pathetic man cowering in the bed of a strange truck, blood trickling from his shoulder. "Manford!" Sarah yelled frantically as she ran toward the truck.

"Don't...I'm not finished!" Manford begged Sarah as tears streamed from his eyes. He stood near the tailgate, still aiming at the large man.

"Help me...he shot me in the shoulder..." Henry cried out in pain. "He's crazy...help me!"

Manford kept the gun aimed at Henry. "Sarah, I'm sorry you had to see this...Henry, the next bullet...is your last!"

Sarah glanced over her shoulder and spotted Conrad step up to Amanda. Amanda put her hands over her mouth and waited for the worst. "Manford...don't kill him!"

Conrad called out. "Let us arrest him and let the law deal with it."

"No! He has to die!" Manford yelled in a miserable voice. "I'll never be able to forgive myself if I don't kill him...my mother will never have peace...I'll never have peace!" Manford looked up into the snow. "I'm not a coward!" he yelled at his old man. "I'm not scared! I won't let him do this to me!"

"Help me!" Henry begged, holding his handcuffed hands over his right shoulder. "He shot me...help me!"

Sarah eased closer to the bed of the truck. "Manford, honey," she said in a soft voice that caused Manford to look down at her finally. "Please—"

"I didn't have anything to do with Mrs. Appleson's murder...I swear," Manford cried. "Sarah...I'm David against Goliath here, just like you told me...and I'm making my mother proud, even though it's too late for her to see me...don't you see? This coward, this evil man, he's proof that I'm innocent. If I kill him, I'm protecting you. I won't let him hurt anyone I love ever, ever again. This is the only way."

Sarah felt tears begin falling from her eyes. Never in her life had she ever felt like a mother to anyone. But now, as she stared at the trembling Manford, his slight figure hunched over the gun, wild eyed as he prepared to kill a monster for many different reasons, she felt a motherly instinct grab her heart and whisper into her soul. "Honey," she said and looked at Henry Billinger in disgust, "he's not worth killing. If you really want justice, let prison eat him alive."

"He has to die...he has to..." Manford cried, ignoring the icy winds and heavy snow slicing into his face.

Sarah, shedding any regard for her life, crawled up into the bed of the truck and placed her hands over the gun Manford was holding. "No, honey, he doesn't," she whispered in Manford's ear. "Sometimes letting a monster live is the best punishment you can issue."

Manford looked up into Sarah's warm, loving eyes and, without fully understanding why, dropped the gun he was holding and threw his arms around her. "Make the pain stop," he begged.

"I will," Sarah promised and pulled Manford into her loving arms.

Conrad looked at Amanda. Amanda tried to speak but couldn't as tears began falling from her own eyes. "I know," he whispered.

Henry, seeing the gun lying at Manford's feet, decided he had one last chance to escape. He slowly lowered his hands and began raising his legs. He had one chance to kick Manford in the back. If he kicked the smaller man just right, his body would fly forward and knock Sarah out of the bed. "Now!" he screamed at the top of his lungs, raised his legs, and kicked Manford square in the back. The impact of the kick threw Manford up against Sarah. Sarah, unable to keep her balance, stumbled backward and fell over the tailgate. She crashed down to the snow and landed hard on her back. Manford didn't go over the back of the tailgate. He threw his hands out, caught his balance, and turned around just as Henry grabbed his gun.

"Time to die, you pathetic little rat!" Henry yelled, aimed the gun at Manford, and began to fire. Before he could squeeze the trigger, a single gunshot sounded. The last thing Henry Billinger remembered before being thrown into an eternal darkness was glancing over to his right and seeing Conrad holding his gun.

"Manford!" Sarah yelled, scrambled to her feet, and looked into the bed of the truck. She spotted Henry Billinger crumpled forward like a rag doll, lying dead at Manford's feet. "Honey...are you okay?"

Manford took his right boot and kicked at Henry. Henry didn't move. He slowly turned his head and looked at Conrad. "I need you around to help me shovel snow," Conrad winked at Manford and put his gun away.

"I'm...okay," Manford said in a shocked voice, finally answering Sarah's frantic questions.

Sarah crawled into the bed of the truck, retrieved the gun, tossed it down into the snow, and then pulled Manford into her arms. "Come on, we're going inside where it's warm."

Manford kicked at Henry's limp form again. "Is he really...dead?"

"Yes."

Manford looked up into Sarah's face. "I was...brave, wasn't I? I mean...I was stupid too, maybe, but I proved my old man wrong...and made my mother proud...I mean...I hoped I made all of you proud of me. Did I?"

Amanda ran up to the bed of the truck and grabbed Manford's hand. "You were so very brave," she cried. "Oh, you sweet little bloke, you were so, so, very brave."

Conrad walked up to the bed of the truck and put out his right hand. "Let me shake the hand of a man whose courage I respect," he smiled as a tear slipped from his eye. "Must be the wind."

Manford looked at Conrad, searched his caring eyes, and then shook his hand. "I guess we might both be watching black and white movies tonight, huh?" he asked.

"You said it," Conrad agreed. He helped Manford down from the truck and then turned his attention to Sarah. "Are you okay?" he asked, assisting Sarah as she climbed down. "You took a hard fall."

"I'm fine," Sarah smiled, gently kissed Conrad, hugged

Amanda, and then kissed Manford's cheek. "My family," she beamed. "All safe."

Manford felt a strange smile touch his face. What was the smile for? Then suddenly he knew: he was smiling because he finally belonged to a family; a family that wanted him not because they felt sorry for him or were obliged to care for him, but because they truly loved him. "Coffee?" he asked.

"You bet," Amanda said and hurried Manford inside.

"Well?" Conrad asked Sarah.

"I think we're going to have to paint the guest room," Sarah smiled, rubbed her sore back, and glanced into the bed of the truck. "That was a clean shot, Detective. I'm impressed. Better call the Chief. Andrew won't be happy about this, even if we did clear up a few mysteries in the process. It's still a dead body," she winced.

Conrad put his arm around Sarah. "Andrew can wait a bit," he said in a tired voice, threw his eyes around at the storm, and shook his head. "How can a place so beautiful attract so many deadly people?" he wondered.

Sarah slid her arm around Conrad's waist, placed her head down on his shoulder, and shook her head. "I don't know, honey. All I do know is that as long as we're a family, no matter what danger awaits us, we'll make it through the storm."

Conrad kissed the top of Sarah's head. "Go on inside and get warm. I'll handle this mess."

"I was hoping you would say that," Sarah smiled. She looked up into Conrad's eyes. "I feel like a mother to him, Conrad."

"I know you do," Conrad smiled.

"What if I mess up?" Sarah asked in a scared voice. "What if I do something wrong and make Manford hate me?"

Conrad lifted his hand and touched the tip of Sarah's nose. "I don't think that's possible. Look," he said and pointed at the cabin. Sarah looked over, spotted Manford standing in the snow, waiting for her. "I think you have a permanent body guard."

Sarah beamed, kissed Conrad, and hurried over to Manford. "Let's go have some coffee."

"I was kinda hoping we could go see Amy afterward," Manford told Sarah. He reached into his coat pocket and pulled out the small tape recorder. "I kinda borrowed the gun and this tape recorder from your office," he explained. "I was hoping...maybe you could play what's on the tape recorder in front of Amy, Amanda and Conrad."

Sarah stared at the tape recorder, took it from Manford,

pressed play, and listened. When the tape ended, she looked down at Manford. "Oh my..."

"I had to do it, Sarah," Manford said, allowing the heavy snow to land on his cold face. "I had to prove to you that I'm innocent...after I realized I was wrong."

"Wrong?"

Manford reached out and took Sarah's hand. "You're not all the same," he told her in an apologetic voice. "Some people really do care."

Sarah bent down, looked deep into Manford's eyes, and smiled. "Like you care about me?" she asked.

Manford felt his cheeks turn red. "Yeah...I do care about you...because I love you."

"And I love you," Sarah whispered, wrapped Manford into her arms, and hugged him tight. It was a hard-won admission from a man who had led a hard life, and she was determined to savor it.

"Enough with the mushy stuff," Amanda yelled from the kitchen door. "Manford, you'd better get in here and walk Mittens before she wets the floor!"

Sarah giggled. "You'll get used to June Bug," she promised.

"I already am," Manford laughed. "Just don't tell her that I love her like a sister...let her figure it out."

"Deal," Sarah laughed and hurried Manford inside.

As she did, Conrad leaned against the bed of the truck, folded his arms, and looked around. "What's next?" he wondered but decided not to worry about it. Instead, he stood in silence for a time and then went to work, calling the Chief of Police and taking care of the crime scene. By the time night arrived, he'd come home exhausted from the long day and crawled into the warm, inviting kitchen.

"I'm home," he announced to Sarah in an exhausted voice, tossed his leather jacket onto the coat rack sitting beside the back door, and looked around the kitchen. The kitchen was empty and quiet. Only a single pizza box, a bottle of root beer, and a lit candle were on the kitchen table. "What's this?"

Sarah, dressed in a lovely blue evening gown, walked over to Conrad, kissed him, and then sat him down at the kitchen table. "Manford and Amy are out on a date," she explained. To Conrad, she smelled like the sweetest roses in the world. "Amanda is at her cabin. Her son called about three hours ago and said he was going to pay her a visit tonight. Seems like he heard about the murders and fires." Sarah sat down across from Conrad. "He's driving down from Fairbanks to check on his dear old mother."

"In other words, we have the night to ourselves?" Conrad asked, feeling like a piece of meatloaf that had been run over a few dozen times but grinning nonetheless.

"Yes, we do," Sarah smiled. "I thought that after you take a long, hot shower, we could sit on the couch and watch movies all night."

"Hey, that's a good plan," Conrad smiled.

Sarah reached into the pizza box, handed Conrad a slice of pizza, took a slice for herself, said a prayer of thanks, and nodded her head. "I also thought we could go to bed early tonight. I feel like I could sleep for a week."

"You and me both," Conrad laughed. He took a bite of his pizza. "But why are you dressed so nice?"

"Oh," Sarah sighed, "because I wanted to feel pretty for you," she explained and kinda blushed. "The world is so ugly, Conrad...it's nice to feel...pretty."

"Is that all?" Conrad asked, reading Sarah's eyes.

"No," Sarah confessed. She looked up at Conrad, felt a tear sting her eye, and forced a sweet smile to her face. "I...wanted to tell you something. Conrad, I want to try and have a child of our own..."

Conrad froze. "You...a child? I..."

"I can see a specialist and see what they say," Sarah winced. "There's still a chance that I can have children...maybe." A tear dropped from Sarah's eyes and landed on her blue evening gown. "I love Manford, honey...and helping to take care of him has made me realize that I want to be a mother. I want a child of my own."

Conrad couldn't believe his ears. Suddenly, he wasn't tired anymore. Suddenly he was terrified out of his boots. "Sarah, I...I mean, we're not getting any younger...and..." Conrad stopped talking, nervously rubbed the back of his neck, and then stood up. "I mean..."

Sarah stood up, walked over to Conrad, and took his hands. "There's a chance that I won't even be able to have children," she explained, as more tears streamed out of her eyes. "But...before that awful snowman who haunts my heart returns...I at least want to try, honey...for us...for the both of us. I want something beautiful in this world. A baby. And Manford, oh, he would make a great big brother...and I think we would make great parents...and Amanda would make a great aunt...and..." Sarah wiped at her tears. "There's too much darkness...too much hate. I need to hear the sound of love and innocence... I need to feel hope around me and...oh honey, the sweet beauty of a baby."

Conrad could clearly see that Sarah was struggling to explain what she was feeling deep inside her heart. He pulled her into his arms and held her. "Okay," he whispered, "we can try...and if it's meant to be...we'll have a beautiful baby," he promised.

Sarah shot her eyes at Conrad in shock. "Really...you

mean it? We can try?" she begged as tears of joy flooded from her eyes.

Conrad nodded his head. "We'll see every specialist in the world if need be."

"Oh...honey!" Sarah exclaimed in absolute joy. "I'm so...I can barely think—thank you! Oh my...I have to tell Amanda." Sarah let go of Conrad and ran to the kitchen phone. Conrad smiled, walked back to the kitchen table, sat down, and picked up his pizza.

"Amanda, guess what...are you sitting down? Good...Conrad and I are going to try and have a baby! ...No, don't come over...your son is on his way...he'll be frantic if you're not home. I...Amanda? Hello? Hello?" Sarah put the phone down and giggled. "Looks like we're having company for—" before Sarah could finish her sentence, she heard Amy and Manford pull up into the driveway in Amy's mother's truck. "Make that three for dinner," she giggled.

Conrad shook his head. "So much for going to bed early tonight," he laughed.

Sarah smiled, opened the back door, and waited for Manford and Amy to appear in the snow. As she stared out into the snow, she saw a hideous snowman appear in the whirling darkness, its leather jacket cruelly familiar, a candy cane in its mouth. *I'll be back, Sarah. You can never kill me...I'll always be around. Be careful, because I'm everywhere...I'm in the darkness...the darkness of people's hearts...*

Sarah felt a cold shiver run down her spine. She shook her head, forced the image of the snowman away, and saw Manford and Amy hurrying through a heavy falling snow. "Maybe you will be back...but I have backup this time," she whispered and touched her stomach where she hoped to soon feel the swell of a baby growing. "And someday...there will be somebody else to fight in my place."

"Who are you talking to?" Manford asked Sarah as he climbed the porch steps, his eyes starry as he escorted his beautiful date home.

"Oh," Sarah replied and smiled down at him, "just myself," she said as the heavy snow continued to fall down onto a sleepy Alaskan town covered in mystery, danger, and...hope.

ABOUT WENDY

Wendy Meadows is the USA Today bestselling author of many novels and novellas, from cozy mysteries to clean, sweet romances. Check out her popular cozy mystery series Sweetfern Harbor, Alaska Cozy and Sweet Peach Bakery, just to name a few.

If you enjoyed this book, please take a few minutes to leave a review. Authors truly appreciate this, and it helps other readers decide if the book might be for them. Thank you!

Get in touch with Wendy
www.wendymeadows.com

amazon.com/author/wendymeadows

goodreads.com/wendymeadows

bookbub.com/authors/wendy-meadows

facebook.com/AuthorWendyMeadows

twitter.com/wmeadowscozy

CPSIA information can be obtained
at www.ICGtesting.com
Printed in the USA
BVHW091354141220
595676BV00014B/2458